'T… a—
M… d in
a…

Indeed. A… oomed, compared to Mrs Brown, Ms Somerville was a bird of paradise. Apart from the coincidences of eye colour and shape this woman bore no resemblance to the woman he'd seen in Mariposa.

Rafe held out his hand. 'Sorry, but for a moment I thought you were someone else. I'm Rafe Peveril.'

Although her lashes flickered, her handshake was as confident as her voice. 'How do you do, Mr Peveril.'

'Most people here call me Rafe,' he told her.

She didn't pretend not to know who he was. 'Of course—you grew up here, didn't you?'

Had there been a glimmer of some other emotion in the sultry green depths of her eyes, almost immediately hidden by those dark lashes?

Rafe's body stirred in a swift, sensually charged response that was purely masculine.

Out of the shop, away from temptation, he reminded himself curtly that he'd long ago got over the adolescent desire to bed every desirable woman he met.

But soon he'd invite Marisa Somerville to dinner.

Robyn Donald can't remember not being able to read, and will be eternally grateful to the local farmers who carefully avoided her on a dusty country road as she read her way to and from school, transported to places and times far away from her small village in Northland, New Zealand. Growing up fed her habit. As well as training as a teacher, marrying and raising two children, she discovered the delights of romances and read them voraciously, especially enjoying the ones written by New Zealand writers. So much so that one day she decided to write one herself. Writing soon grew to be as much of a delight as reading—although infinitely more challenging—and when eventually her first book was accepted by Mills & Boon she felt she'd arrived home.

She still lives in a small town in Northland, with her family close by, using the landscape as a setting for much of her work. Her life is enriched by the friends she's made among writers and readers, and complicated by a determined Corgi called Buster, who is convinced that blackbirds are evil entities. Her greatest hobby is still reading, with travelling a very close second.

Recent titles by the same author:

ONE NIGHT IN THE ORIENT
(One Night In…)
THE FAR SIDE OF PARADISE
POWERFUL GREEK, HOUSE KEEPER WIFE
(The Greek Tycoons)

STEPPING OUT OF THE SHADOWS

BY

ROBYN DONALD

All the characters in this book have no existence outside the imagination of the author, and have no relation whatsoever to anyone bearing the same name or names. They are not even distantly inspired by any individual known or unknown to the author, and all the incidents are pure invention.

First published in Great Britain 2012
by Mills & Boon, an imprint of Harlequin (UK) Limited.
Harlequin (UK) Limited, Eton House, 18-24 Paradise Road,
Richmond, Surrey TW9 1SR

ISBN: 978 0 263 89061 7

Harlequin (UK) policy is to use papers that are natural, renewable and recyclable products and made from wood grown in sustainable forests. The logging and manufacturing process conform to the legal environmental regulations of the country of origin.

Printed and bound in Spain
by Blackprint CPI, Barcelona

STEPPING OUT OF THE SHADOWS

CHAPTER ONE

HEART thudding more noisily than the small plane's faltering engine, Rafe Peveril dragged his gaze away from the rain-lashed windows, no longer able to see the darkening grasslands of Mariposa beneath them. A few seconds ago, just after the engine had first spluttered, he'd noticed a hut down there.

If they made it out of this alive, that hut might be their only hope of surviving the night.

Another violent gust of wind shook the plane. The engine coughed a couple of times, then failed. In the eerie silence the pilot muttered a jumble of prayers and curses in his native Spanish as he fought to keep the plane steady.

If they were lucky—*damned* lucky—they might land more or less intact…

When the engines sputtered back into life the woman beside Rafe looked up, white face dominated by great green eyes, black-lashed and tip-tilted and filled with fear.

Thank God she wasn't screaming. He reached for her hand, gave it a quick hard squeeze, then released it to push her head down.

"Brace position," he shouted, his voice far too loud in the sudden silence as the engines stopped again. The woman huddled low and Rafe set his teeth and steeled himself for the crash.

A shuddering jolt, a whirlwind of noise…

And Rafe woke.

Jerking upright, he let out a sharp breath, grey eyes sweeping a familiar room. The adrenalin surging through him mutated into relief. Instead of regaining consciousness in a South American hospital bed he was at home in his own room in New Zealand.

What the *hell…*?

It had to be at least a couple of years since he'd relived the crash. He searched for a trigger that could have summoned the dream but his memory—usually sharply accurate—failed him.

Again.

Six years should have accustomed him to the blank space in his head after the crash, yet although he'd given up on futile attempts to remember, he still resented those forty-eight vanished hours.

The bedside clock informed him that sunrise was too close to try for any more sleep—not that he'd manage it now. He needed space and fresh air.

Outside on the terrace he inhaled deeply, relishing the mingled scent of salt and flowers and newly mown grass, and the quiet hush of the waves. His heart rate slowed and the memories receded into the past where they belonged. Light from a fading moon surrounded the house with mysterious shadows, enhanced by the bright disc of Venus hanging above a bar of pure gold along the horizon where the sea met the sky.

The Mariposan pilot had died on impact, but miraculously both he and the wife of his estancia manager had survived with minor injures—the blow to the head for him, and apparently nothing more serious than a few bruises for her.

With some difficulty he conjured a picture of the woman—a drab nonentity, hardly more than a girl. Although he'd spent the night before the crash at the estancia, she'd kept very much in the background while he and her husband talked business. All he could recall were those amazingly green eyes in her otherwise forgettable face. Apart from them, she had been a plain woman.

With a plain name—Mary Brown.

He couldn't recall seeing her smile—not that that was surprising. A week or so before he'd arrived at the estancia she'd received news of her mother's sudden stroke and resultant paralysis. As soon as Rafe heard about it he'd offered to take her back with him to Mariposa's capital and organise a flight to New Zealand.

Rafe frowned. What the hell was her husband's name?

He recalled it with an odd sense of relief. David Brown—another plain name, and the reason for Rafe's trip to Mariposa. He'd broken his flight home from London to see for himself if he agreed with the Mariposan agent's warnings that David Brown was not a good fit for the situation.

Certainly Brown's response to his offer to escort his wife back to New Zealand had been surprising.

"That won't be necessary," David Brown had told him brusquely. "She's been ill—she doesn't need the extra stress of looking after a cripple."

However, by the next morning the man had changed his mind, presumably at his wife's insistence, and that evening she'd accompanied Rafe on the first stage of the trip.

An hour after take-off they'd been caught by a wind of startling ferocity, and with it came rain so cold the woman beside him had been shivering within minutes. And the plane's engines had cut out for the first time.

If it hadn't been for the skill of the doomed pilot they'd probably all have died.

Of course! There was the stimulus—the trigger that had hurled his dreaming mind back six years.

Rafe inhaled sharply, recalling the email that had arrived just before he'd gone to bed last night. Sent from his office in London, for the first time in recorded history his efficient personal assistant had slipped up. No message, just a forwarded photograph of a dark young man wearing a look of conscious pride and a mortarboard, a graduation shot. Amused by his PA's omission, Rafe had sent back one question mark.

Last night he hadn't made the connection, but the kid looked very much like the pilot.

He swung around and headed for his office, switched on the computer, waited impatiently for it to boot up and smiled ironically when he saw another email.

His PA had written, *Sorry about the stuff-up. I've just had a letter from the widow of the pilot in Mariposa. Apparently you promised their oldest boy an interview with the organisation there when he graduated from university. Photo of good-looking kid in mortarboard attached. OK to organise?*

So that explained the dream. Rafe's subconscious had made the connection for him in a very forthright fashion. He'd felt a certain obligation to the family of the dead pilot and made it his business to help them.

He replied with a succinct agreement to London, then headed back to his bedroom to dress.

After a gruelling trip to several African countries, it

was great to be home, and apart from good sex and the exhilaration of business there was little he liked better than a ride along the beach on his big bay gelding in a Northland summer dawn.

Perhaps it might give him some inspiration for the gift he needed to buy that day, a birthday present for his foster-sister. His mouth curved. Gina had forthright views on appropriate gifts for a modern young woman.

"You might be a plutocrat," she'd told him the day before, "but don't you dare get your secretary to buy me something flashy and glittering. I don't do glitter."

He'd pointed out that his middle-aged PA would have been insulted to hear herself described as a secretary, and added that any presents he bought were his own choice, no one else's.

Gina grinned and gave him a sisterly punch in the arm. "Oh, yeah? So why did you get me to check the kiss-off present you gave your last girlfriend?"

"It was her birthday gift," he contradicted. "And if I remember correctly, you insisted on seeing it."

She arched an eyebrow. "Of course I did. So it was just a coincidence you broke off the affair a week later?"

"It was a mutual decision," Rafe told her, the touch of frost in his tone a warning.

His private life was his own. Because he had no desire to cause grief he chose his lovers for sophistication as well as their appeal to his mind and his senses. Eventually he intended to marry.

One day.

"Well, I suppose the diamonds salvaged a bit of pride for her," Gina had observed cynically, hugging him before getting into her car for the trip back to Auckland. She'd turned on the engine, then said casually through the open window, "If you're looking for something a bit different, the gift shop in Tewaka has a new owner. It's got some really good stuff in it now."

Recognising a hint when he heard one, several hours later Rafe headed for the small seaside town twenty kilometres from the homestead.

Inside the gift shop he looked around. Gina was right—the place had been fitted out with taste and style. His appreciative gaze took in demure yet sexy lingerie displayed with discretion, frivolous sandals perfect for any four-year-old girl who yearned to be a princess, some very good New Zealand art glass. As well as clothes there were ornaments and jewellery, even some books. And art, ranging in style from brightly coloured coastal scenes to moody, dramatic oils.

"Can I help you?"

Rafe swivelled around, met the shop assistant's eyes and felt the ground shift beneath his feet. Boldly green and cat-tilted, set between lashes thick enough to tangle any heart, they sent him spinning back to his dream.

"Mary?" he asked without thinking.

But of course she wasn't Mary Brown.

This woman was far from plain and an involuntary glance showed no ring on those long fingers. Although her eyes were an identical green, they were bright and challenging, not dully unaware.

Her lashes drooped and he sensed her subtle—but very definite—withdrawal.

"I'm sorry—have we met before?" she asked in an assured, crisp voice completely unlike Mary Brown's hesitant tone. She added with a smile, "But my name isn't Mary. It's Marisa—Marisa Somerville."

Indeed, the assured, beautifully groomed Ms Somerville was a bird of paradise compared to drab Mrs Brown. Apart from the coincidences of eye colour and shape, and first names beginning with the same letter, this woman bore no resemblance to the woman he'd seen in Mariposa.

Rafe held out his hand. "Sorry, but for a moment I thought you were someone else. I'm Rafe Peveril."

Although her lashes flickered, her handshake was as confident as her voice. "How do you do, Mr Peveril."

"Most people here call me Rafe," he told her.

She didn't pretend not to know who he was. Had there been a glimmer of some other emotion in the sultry green depths of her eyes, almost immediately hidden by those dark lashes?

If so, he could hear no sign of it in her voice when she went on, "Would you rather look around by yourself, or can I help you in any way?"

She hadn't granted him permission to use her first name. Intrigued, and wryly amused at his reaction to her unspoken refusal, Rafe said, "My sister is having a birthday soon, and from the way she spoke of your shop I gathered she'd seen something here she liked. Do you know Gina Smythe?"

"Everyone in Tewaka knows Gina." Smiling, she turned towards one of the side walls. "And, yes, I can tell you what she liked."

"Gina isn't noted for subtlety," he said drily, appreciating the gentle feminine sway of slender hips, the graceful smoothness of her gait. His body stirred in a swift, sensually charged response that was purely masculine.

She stopped in front of an abstract oil. "This is the one."

Rafe dragged his mind back to his reason for being there. Odd that Gina, so practical and matter-of-fact, couldn't resist art that appealed directly to the darker, more stormy emotions.

"Who's the artist?" he asked after a silent moment.

The woman beside him gave a soft laugh. "I am," she admitted.

The hot tug of lust in Rafe's gut intensified, startling him. Was she as passionate as the painting before him? Perhaps he'd find out some day…

"I'll take it," he said briskly. "Can you gift-wrap it for me? I'll call back in half an hour."

"Yes, of course."

"Thanks."

Out of the shop, away from temptation, he reminded himself curtly that he'd long ago got over the adolescent desire to bed every desirable woman he met. Yet primitive hunger still quickened his blood.

Soon he'd invite Marisa Somerville to dinner.

If she was unattached, which seemed unlikely in spite of her ringless fingers. Women who looked like her—especially ones who exuded that subtle sexuality—usually had a man in the not-very-distant background.

Probably, he thought cynically, stopping to speak to a middle-aged woman he'd known from childhood, he'd responded to her so swiftly because it was several months since he'd made love.

From behind the flimsy barrier of the sales counter Marisa watched him, her pulse still hammering so loudly in her ears she hardly heard the rising shriek of the siren at the local fire-brigade headquarters.

She resisted the impulse to go and wash Rafe Peveril's grip from her skin. A handshake was meant to be impersonal, an unthreatening gesture…

Yet when he'd taken her outstretched hand in his strong, tempered fingers an erotic shiver had sizzled through every cell. Rafe Peveril's touch had been unbearably stimulating, as dangerous as a siren's song.

If a simple, unemotional handshake could do that, what would happen if he kissed her—?

Whoa! Outraged, she ordered her wayward mind to shut down that train of thought.

For two months she'd been bracing herself for this—ever since she'd been appalled to discover Rafe Peveril lived not far from Tewaka. Yet when she'd looked up to see him pace into the shop, more than six foot of intimidating authority and leashed male force, she'd had to stop herself from bolting out the back door.

Of all the rotten coincidences… It hadn't occurred to her to check the names of the local bigwigs before signing the contract that locked her into a year's lease of the shop.

She should have followed her first impulse after her father's death and crossed the Tasman Sea to take refuge in Australia.

At least her luck had held—Rafe hadn't recognised her. It was difficult to read the brilliant mind behind his arrogantly autocratic features, but she'd be prepared to bet that after a jolt of what might have been recognition he'd completely accepted her new persona and identity.

She swallowed hard as the fire engine raced past, siren screaming. Please God it was just a grass fire, not a motor accident, or someone's house.

Her gaze fell to the picture she'd just sold. Forcing herself to breathe carefully and steadily, she took it off the wall and carried it across to the counter.

Gina Smythe was the sort of woman Marisa aspired to be—self-assured, decisive, charming. But of course

Rafe Peveril's sister would have been born with the same effortless, almost ruthless self-confidence that made him so intimidating.

Whereas it had taken her years—and much effort—to manufacture the façade she now hid behind. Only she knew that deep inside her lurked the naive, foolish kid filled with simple-minded hope and fairytale fantasies who'd married David Brown and gone with him to Mariposa, expecting an exotic tropical paradise and the romance of a lifetime.

Her mouth curved in a cynical, unamused line as she expertly cut a length of gift-wrapping paper.

How wrong she'd been.

However, that was behind her now. And as she couldn't get out of her lease agreement, she'd just have to make sure everyone—especially Rafe Peveril—saw her as the woman who owned the best gift shop in Northland.

She had to make a success of this venture and squirrel away every cent she could. Once the year was up she'd leave Tewaka for somewhere safer—a place where her past didn't intrude and she could live without fear, a place where she could at last settle.

The sort of place she thought she'd found in Tewaka…

Half an hour later she was keeping a wary eye on the entrance while dealing with a diffident middle-aged woman who couldn't make up her mind. Every suggestion was met with a vague comment that implied rejection.

Once, Marisa thought compassionately, she'd been like that. Perhaps this woman too was stuck in a situation with no escape. Curbing her tension, she walked her around the shop, discussing the recipient of the proposed gift, a fourteen-year-old girl who seemed to terrify her grandmother.

A movement from the door made her suck in an involuntary breath as Rafe Peveril strode in, his size and air of cool authority reducing the shop and its contents to insignificance.

Black-haired, tanned and arrogantly handsome, his broad-shouldered, narrow-hipped body moving in a lithe predator's gait on long, heavily muscled legs, he was a man who commanded instant attention.

Naked, he was even more magnificent...

Appalled by the swift memory from a past she'd tried very hard to forget, she murmured, "If you don't mind, I'll give Mr Peveril his parcel."

"Oh, yes—do." The customer looked across the shop, turning faintly pink when she received a smile that sizzled with male charisma.

Deliberately relaxing her taut muscles, Marisa set off towards him. He knew the effect that smile had on women.

It set female hearts throbbing—as hers was right now.

Not, however, solely with appreciation.

In Mariposa his height had struck her first. Only when he'd been close had she noticed that his eyes were grey, so dark they were the colour of iron.

But in Mariposa his gaze had been coolly aloof.

Now he made no attempt to hide his appreciation. Heat licked through her, warring with a primitive sense of approaching danger. She forced a smile, hoping he'd take the mechanical curve of her lips for genuine pleasure.

"Hello, Mr Peveril, here's your parcel," she said, lowering her lashes as she placed it carefully on the counter.

"Thank you." After a quick look he asked, "Do you give lessons in parcel wrapping and decoration?"

Startled, she looked up, parrying his direct, keen survey with a mildly enquiring lift of her brows. "I hadn't thought of it."

A long finger tapped the parcel. "This is beautifully done. With Christmas not too far away you'd probably have plenty of takers."

Easy chitchat was not his style. He'd been pleasant enough in Mariposa, but very much the boss—

Don't think of Mariposa.

It was stupid to feel that somehow her wayward thoughts might show in her face and trigger a vagrant memory in him.

Stupid and oddly scary. It took a lot of will to look him in the eye and say in a steady voice, "Thank you. I might put a notice in the window and see what happens."

As though he'd read her mind, he said in an idle tone at variance with his cool, keen scrutiny, "I have this odd feeling we've met before, but I'm certain I'd remember if we had."

Oh, God! Calling on every ounce of self-preservation, she said brightly, "So would I, Mr Peveril—"

"Rafe."

She swallowed. Her countrymen were famously casual, so it was stupid to feel that using his first name forged some sort of link. "Rafe," she repeated, adding with another meaningless smile, "I'd have remembered too, I'm sure." Oh, hell, did that sound like an attempt at flirtation? Hastily she added, "I do hope your sister enjoys the painting."

"I'm sure she will. Thank you." He nodded, picked up the parcel and left.

Almost giddy with relief, Marisa had to take a couple of deep breaths before she returned to her customer. It took another ten minutes before the woman finally made up her mind, and while Marisa was wrapping the gift, she leaned forwards and confided in a low voice, "Gina Smythe's not really Rafe's sister, you know."

"No, I didn't know." Marisa disliked gossip, so she tried to make her tone brisk and dismissive even though curiosity assailed her.

"Poor girl, she was in a foster home not far from here—one she didn't like—so she ran away when she was about six and hid in a cave on Manuwai."

At Marisa's uncomprehending glance she elaborated, "Manuwai is the Peveril station, out on the coast north of here. The family settled there in the very early days. It's one of the few land grants still intact—an enormous place. Rafe found Gina and took her home with him, and his parents more or less adopted her. Rafe's an only child."

"Ah, I see." No wonder Gina and Rafe didn't share a surname.

And she'd been so sure the woman's sense of confidence had been born in her…

The woman leaned closer. "When I say his parents, it was his stepmother, really. His *birth* mother left him and his father when Rafe was about six. It was a great scandal—she divorced him and married a film star, then divorced him and married someone else—and it was rumoured the elder Mr Peveril paid millions of dollars to get rid of her."

Shocked, Marisa tried to cut her off, only to have the woman drop her voice even further. "She was very beautiful—always dashing off to Auckland and Australia and going on cruises and trips to Bali." Her tone made that exotic island paradise sound like one of the nether regions of hell.

Hoping to put an end to this, Marisa handed over the purchase in one of her specially designed bags. "Thank you," she said firmly.

But the woman was not to be deterred. "She didn't even look after Rafe—he had a nanny from the time he was born. His stepmother—the second Mrs Peveril—was very nice, but she couldn't have children, so Rafe is an only child. Such a shame..."

Her voice trailed away when another customer entered the shop. Intensely relieved, Marisa grabbed the opportunity. "I'm pretty certain your granddaughter will love this, but if she doesn't, come back with her and we'll find something she does like."

"That's very kind of you," the woman fluttered. "Thank you very much, my dear."

The rest of the day was too busy for Marisa to think about what she'd heard, and once she'd closed the shop she walked along the street to the local after-school centre. She'd chosen Tewaka to settle in for various reasons, but that excellent care centre had been the clincher.

Her heart swelled at the grin from her son. "Hello, darling. How's your day been?"

"Good," he told her, beaming as he always did. To five-year-old Keir every day was good. How had Rafe Peveril's days been after his mother had left?

Keir asked, "Did you have a good day too?"

She nodded. "Yes, a cruise ship—a really big one—came into the Bay of Islands, so I had plenty of customers." And most had bought something.

Fishing around in his bag, Keir asked, "Can I go to Andy's birthday party? Please," he added conscientiously. "He gave me this today." He handed over a somewhat crumpled envelope.

Taking it, she thought wryly that in a way it was a pity he'd settled so well. A sunny, confident boy, he'd made friends instantly and he was going to miss them when they left. "I'll read it when we get home, but I don't see any reason why not."

He beamed again, chattering almost nonstop while they shopped in the supermarket. Marisa's heart swelled, then contracted into a hard ball in her chest. Keir was her reason for living, the pivot of her life. His welfare was behind every decision she'd made since the day she'd realised she was pregnant.

No matter what it took, she'd make sure he had everything he needed to make him happy.

And that, she thought later after a tussle of wills had seen him into bed, included discipline.

Whatever else he missed out on, he had a mother who loved him. Which, if local gossip was anything to go by, was more than Rafe Peveril had had. He'd only been a year older than Keir when his mother had left.

She felt a huge compassion for the child he'd been. Had that first great desertion made him the tough, ruthless man he was now?

More than likely. But although the sad story gave her a whole new perspective on him, she'd be wise to remember she was dealing with the man he was now, not the small deserted boy he'd once been.

That night memories of his hard, speculative survey kept her awake. She hated to think of the way she'd been when she'd first met him—ground down into a grey shadow of a woman—and she'd been hugely relieved when he didn't recognise her.

Images sharpened by a primitive fear flooded back, clear and savagely painful. Two years of marriage to David had almost crushed her.

If it hadn't been for Rafe Peveril she'd probably still be on that lonely estancia in Mariposa, unable to summon the strength—or the courage, she thought with an involuntary tightening of her stomach muscles—to get away.

It had taken several years and a lot of effort to emerge from that dark world of depression and insecurity. Now she had the responsibility of her son, she'd never again trust herself to a man with an urge to dominate.

Twisting in her bed, she knew she wasn't going to sleep. She had no camomile tea, but a cup of the peppermint variety might soothe her enough.

Even as she stood in the darkened kitchen of the little, elderly cottage she rented, a mug of peppermint tea in hand, she knew it wasn't going to work. She grimaced as she gazed out into the summer night—one made for lovers, an evocation of all that was romantic, the moon's silver glamour spreading a shimmering veil of magic over the countryside.

Bewildered by an inchoate longing for something unknown, something *more*—something primal and consuming and intense—she was almost relieved when hot liquid sloshed on to her fingers, jerking her back into real life.

Hastily she set the mug on the bench and ran cold water over her hand until the mild stinging stopped.

"That's what you get for staring at the moon," she muttered and, picking up her mug again, turned away from the window.

Seeing Rafe Peveril again had set off a reckless energy, as though her body had sprung to life after a long sleep.

She should have expected it.

Her first sight of him at the estancia, climbing down from the old Jeep, had awakened a determination she'd thought she'd lost. His raw male vitality—forceful yet disciplined—had broken through her grey apathy.

From somewhere she'd summoned the initiative to tell him of her mother's illness and that she wasn't expected to live.

Then, when David had refused Rafe's offer to take her home, she'd gathered every ounce of courage and defied him.

She shivered. Thank heavens she was no longer that frail, damaged woman. Now, it seemed incredible she'd let herself get into such a state.

Instead of standing in the dark recalling the crash, she should be exulting, joyously relieved because the meeting she'd been dreading for the past two months had happened without disaster.

Oh, Rafe had noticed her, all right—but only with masculine interest.

So she'd passed the first big hurdle. *If only she could get rid of the nagging instinct that told her to run. Now—while she still could.*

What if he eventually worked out that she and Mary Brown were the same woman?

What if David was still working for him, and he told her ex-husband where she and Keir were?

What if he found out about the lie she'd told David—the lie that had finally and for ever freed her and her son?

Marisa took another deep breath and drained the mug

of lukewarm tea. That wasn't going to happen because her ex-husband didn't care about Keir.

Anyway, worrying was a waste of time and nervous energy. All she had to do was avoid Rafe Peveril, which shouldn't be difficult, even in a place as small as Tewaka—his vast empire kept him away for much of the time.

Closing the curtains on the sultry enchantment of the moon, she tried to feel reassured. While she kept out of his way she'd make plans for a future a long way from Tewaka.

Somewhere safe—where she could start again.

Start again...

She'd believed—hoped—she'd done that for the last time when she'd arrived in Tewaka. A soul-deep loneliness ached through her. Her life had been nothing but new starts.

Sternly she ordered herself not to wallow in self-pity. Before she decided to put down roots again, she'd check out the locals carefully.

Also, she thought ruefully, if she could manage it she'd buy some dull-brown contact lenses.

CHAPTER TWO

TO SAVE money, Keir stayed at the shop after school two days each week. He enjoyed chatting to customers and playing with toys in the tiny office at the back.

Which was where he was when Marisa heard a deep, hard voice. Her heart thudded painfully in her chest.

Rafe Peveril. It had been almost a week since he'd bought the gift for his sister, and she'd just started to relax. *Please*, let him buy another one and then go away and never come back, she begged the universe.

In vain. Without preamble he asked, "Do you, by any chance, have a relative named Mary Brown?"

Panic froze her breath. Desperately she said the first thing that wasn't a lie, hoping he didn't recognise it for an evasion. "As far as I know I have no female relatives. Certainly not one called Mary Brown. Why?"

And allowed her gaze to drift enquiringly upwards from the stock she was checking. Something very close to terror hollowed out her stomach. He was watching her far too closely, the striking framework of his face very prominent, his gaze narrowed and unreadable.

From the corner of her eye she saw the office door slide open. Her heart stopped in her chest.

Keir, stay there, she begged silently.

But her son wandered out, his expression alert yet a

little wary as he stared up at the man beside his mother. “Mummy…” he began, not quite tentatively.

“Not now, darling.” Marisa struggled to keep her voice steady and serene. “I’ll be with you in a minute.”

He sent her a resigned look, but turned to go back, stopping only when Rafe Peveril said in a voice edged by some emotion she couldn’t discern, “I can wait.” He looked down at Keir. “Hello, I’m Rafe Peveril. What’s your name?”

“Keir,” her son told him, always ready to talk to adults.

“Keir who?”

Keir’s face crinkled into laughter. “Not Keir Who—I’m Keir Somerville—”

Abruptly, Marisa broke in. “Off you go, Keir.”

But Rafe said, “He’s all right. How old are you, Keir?”

“I’m five,” Keir told him importantly. “I go to school now.”

“Who is your teacher?”

“Mrs Harcourt,” Keir said. “She’s got a dog and a kitten, and yesterday she brought the kitty to school.” He shot a glance at Marisa before fixing his gaze back on the compellingly handsome face of the man who watched him. “I want a puppy but Mum says not yet ’cause we’d have to leave him by himself and he’d be lonely all day, but another lady has a shop too, and she’s got a little dog and her dog sleeps on a cushion in the shop with her and it’s happy all day.”

And then, thank heavens, another customer came in and Marisa said evenly, “Off you go, Keir.”

With obvious reluctance Keir headed away, but not before giving Rafe a swift smile and saying, “Goodbye, Mr Pev’ril.”

Rafe watched until he was out of hearing before transferring his gaze to Marisa's face. "A pleasant child."

"Thank you," she said automatically, still spooked by the speculation in his hard scrutiny. "Can I help you at all?"

"No, I just came in to tell you I'm now very high in my sister's favour. When I told her you had painted the picture she was surprised and wondered why you hadn't signed it. We could only make out your initials."

She couldn't tell him the last thing she wanted was her name where someone who knew her—or David—might see it. So she smiled and shrugged. "I don't really know—I just never have."

He appeared to take that at face value. "She asked me to tell you that she loves it and is over the moon."

Marisa relaxed a little. "That's great," she said. "Thank your sister from me, please."

"She'll probably come in and enthuse about it herself when she's next up, so I'll leave that to you." His matter-of-fact tone dismissed her, reinforced by his rapid glance at the clock at the back of the shop. "I have to go, but we'll meet again."

Not if I see you first, Marisa thought uneasily, but managed to say, "I'm sure we will."

Parrying another hard glance with her most limpid smile, she tried to ignore her jumping nerve-ends as she moved away to deal with another customer, who'd decided to begin Christmas shopping.

Surprisingly for an afternoon, a steady stream of shoppers kept her so busy she had no time to mull over Rafe's unexpected visit or the even more unexpected attention he'd paid to her son.

Or her reckless—and most unusual—response to

him. It had absolutely nothing to do with the fact that she'd slept entwined in his arms, heart to heart, her legs tangled in his, her skin warming him…

Get out of my head, she ordered the intrusive memories.

Later, after they'd got home, she hung out a load of washing, trying to convince herself that her apprehension was without foundation. A wistful pain jagged through her as she watched Keir tear around on the bicycle that had been her father's final gift to him.

It was foolish to be so alarmed by Rafe Peveril. He was no threat to her or—more important—to Keir.

Because even if her ex-husband was still working for the Peveril organisation, she no longer needed to fear David. Not for herself, anyway… She was a different woman from the green girl who'd married him. She'd suffered and been lost, and eventually realised that the only way she'd survive was to rescue herself.

And she'd done it. Now she had a life and the future she'd crafted for herself and her son. She'd let no one—certainly not Rafe Peveril—take that from her.

Yet for the rest of the day darkness clouded her thoughts, dragging with it old fear, old pain and memories of will-sapping despair at being trapped in a situation she'd been unable to escape.

Because there was the ugly matter of the lie—the one that had won her freedom and Keir's safety.

Unseeingly, Rafe frowned at the glorious view from his office window, remembering black-lashed eyes and silky skin—skin that had paled that afternoon when Marisa Somerville had looked up and seen him. Her hands, elegant, capable and undecorated by rings had stiffened for a few seconds, and then trembled slightly.

A nagging sense of familiarity taunted him, refusing to be dismissed. Yet it had to be just the random coincidence of eye colour and shape. Apart from those eyes, nothing connected Marisa Somerville to the drab nonentity who had been married to David Brown.

Marisa was everything poor Mary Brown wasn't.

He let his memory range from glossy hair the colour of dark honey to satiny skin with a subtle sheen, and a mouth that beckoned with generous sensuality.

A sleeping hunger stirred, one so fiercely male and sharply focused it refused to be dismissed.

So, Marisa Somerville was very attractive.

Hell, how inadequate was that? he thought with a cynical smile. His recollection of a body that even her restrained clothes hadn't been able to subdue prompted him to add *sexy* to *attractive.*

It hadn't been simple recognition that had shadowed that tilted, siren's gaze. His frown deepened. He considered himself an astute judge of reactions and in any other situation he'd have guessed Marisa's had come very close to fear…

Only for a second. She'd recovered fast, although a hint of tension had reappeared when her son had entered the shop.

Possibly what he'd seen in Marisa Somerville's face was nothing more than a feminine resistance to the basic, sexual pull between a fertile woman and a virile man—a matter of genes recognising a possible mate—a pull he'd also felt.

Still did, he realised, drily amused by his hardening body.

That certainly hadn't happened in Mariposa, when

he'd met Mary Brown. She'd looked at him with no expression, shaken his hand as though forced to and immediately faded into the background. What *had* lodged in his mind had been the dislocating contrast between fascinating eyes and the rest of her—thin, listless, her dragging voice, sallow skin and the lank hair of pure mouse scraped back from her face into a ponytail.

Rafe looked around his office, letting the warmth and practicality of the room soak into him.

This room represented the essence of his life; five generations of Peveril men and women had sat behind the huge kauri desk and worked to create the superbly productive empire that had expanded from a wilderness to encompass the world.

He hoped one day a son or daughter of his would occupy the same chair behind the same desk, with the same aim—to feed as many people as he could.

His father had set up an organisation to help the Mariposan government introduce modern farming practices, but after his death Rafe had discovered a chaotic state of affairs. That first, fact-finding trip to Mariposa had been the impetus to impose a proper chain of control, a process that involved total restructuring as well as hiring a workforce he could trust.

He made an impatient gesture and turned to the computer. He had more important things to think about than a possible—if unlikely—link between Marisa Somerville and the wife of one of his farm managers.

Yet he couldn't dislodge the memory of that flash of recognition and the fleeting, almost haunted expression in Marisa's eyes.

Although Rafe rarely had hunches, preferring to follow his logical brain, when they did occur he'd learned to stick with them. A self-derisive smile curving his mouth, he checked the time in Mariposa, then picked up the telephone.

His agent there was surprised at his question, but answered readily enough, "I was not part of this organisation then, you remember, but of course I do recall the circumstances. It was in the newspapers. Señor Brown burned down the machinery shed on that estancia. One of the farmhands almost died in the fire. I understand he was given the chance to leave or be handed over to the police. He left."

Brows drawing even closer together, Rafe demanded, "Why was I not told of this?"

"I do not know."

In fact, it was just another example of the previous agent's inefficiency. Mouth compressing into a thin line, Rafe said, "Of course you don't. Sorry. When did this sabotage happen?"

There was a pause, then the manager said a little stiffly, "I will need to check the exact date, you understand, but it was a few weeks after you and Mrs Brown left for New Zealand."

Rafe's gaze narrowed. The phrase probably indicated only that English wasn't his agent's first language. Technically true, but not in the way it seemed to indicate.

But if David Brown had thought…?

With a sardonic smile Rafe dismissed the idea.

However, it kept recurring during the following week as he hosted an overseas delegation, wining and dining them before intensive discussions that ended very satisfactorily.

He celebrated by taking an old flame out to dinner, tactfully declining her oblique suggestion they spend the night together. Although he was fond of her and they'd enjoyed a satisfying affair some years previously, he was no longer interested. And was irritated when a roving photographer snapped them together as they left the reception. New Zealand had nothing like the paparazzi overseas, but the photograph appeared in the social news of one of the Sunday papers the next day.

Back at Manuwai he found himself reaching for the telephone, only to realise that it was the weekend and he didn't know Marisa Somerville's number. It wasn't in the telephone book either.

And why did he want to ring her? Because she reminded him of another woman?

Grimly, he recalled what he could of the day he and Mary Brown had left the estancia, little more than irritating flashes and fragments—more sensation than sight—of the storm that had brought the plane down. Even after he'd woken in the hospital bed, fully aware once more, he'd remembered nothing of the aftermath.

He'd been told that Mary Brown had brought him to the hut, that she'd probably saved his life…

And without warning a flash of memory returned—a quiet voice, his gratitude at the warmth of arms around him…

That was all. Rafe swore and got to his feet, pacing across the room to stand at the window. He took a few deliberate breaths, willing his racing thoughts to slow. Why hadn't he remembered that before?

Had the sight of a pair of black-lashed green eyes prodded this elusive fragment from his reluctant brain?

After he'd been released from hospital both he and Mary Brown had travelled to New Zealand in a private jet with a nurse in attendance—a flight he barely remembered, though obviously it had set the gossips in Mariposa buzzing.

Well, let them think what they liked. He never pursued committed women, no matter how alluring.

Ignoring the flame of anticipation that licked through him, Rafe shrugged. He'd find out whether Marisa Somerville was in a relationship soon enough. Tewaka also had gossips, and information inevitably found its way to him.

Keir said fretfully, "Mummy, I don't want you to go out." He thought a moment before adding, "I might feel sick if you do."

At his mother's look he grinned. "Well, I *might*."

"You won't, my darling. I'll be here when you wake up tomorrow morning and you'll be fine with Tracey. And tomorrow is Saturday, so you can come into the shop with me."

Keir knew when persistence could—occasionally—be rewarded and also when to give up. The sigh he heaved was heartfelt, but the prospect of an ice cream muted its full force. "I like Tracey."

"I know. And here she comes now."

But Marisa couldn't repress a few motherly qualms as she drove away. Although her landlord's daughter—a seventeen-year-old with two younger brothers—was both competent and practical, with her mother available only a couple of hundred metres along the road, Marisa had never before gone out and left Keir to be put to bed.

However, taking part in this weekly get-together of local business people was something she'd been promising herself. If nothing else it would expand her circle of contacts and she needed to take every opportunity to make her shop a success.

Nevertheless, she felt a little tense when she walked into the room, and even more so when the bustling, middle-aged convener confided, "We're honoured tonight—normally we don't have speakers, but this afternoon I talked Rafe Peveril into giving us his ideas about how he sees the future of Northland and Tewaka."

"Oh, that should be interesting," Marisa said with a bright, false smile that hid, she hoped, her sudden urge to get out of there.

Ten days should have given her time to get over the impact of meeting him again, but it hadn't. Five minutes later she was producing that same smile as the convener began to introduce Rafe to her.

Smoothly he cut in, "Ms Somerville and I have already met."

"Oh, good," the convener said, not without an interested note in her voice.

Somehow Marisa found herself beside Rafe with her hard-won poise rapidly leaking away.

"I believe you're living in the Tanners' farm cottage," he said.

Of course anyone who was interested—and quite a few who weren't—would know. Marisa said briskly, "Yes, it's very convenient." And cheap.

"So who's looking after your son tonight?"

Slightly startled, she looked up, brows raised. "That's part of the convenience. Tracey—the Tanners' daughter—is more than happy to babysit. She and Keir get on well together."

He nodded, dark head inclining slightly towards her, grey eyes cool and assessing. A rebel response—heady and heated in the pit of her stomach—caught her by surprise.

"I hadn't realised this is the first time you've come to one of these meetings," he said.

"I've been intending to, but…" Shrugging, she let the words trail away.

"Point out the people you don't know."

Surprised again, she did so, wondering if he was using this method to politely move away. However, although he introduced her to everyone she indicated, he stayed beside her until it was time for him to speak.

Good manners, she thought stoutly, nothing more. Dragging her mind back to what he was saying, she realised that the quality of Rafe Peveril's mind shone through his incisive words and she liked the flashes of humour that added to both his talk and his answers to questions afterwards.

Reluctantly, she was impressed. Although his family had an assured position in the district, it was a long climb from New Zealand to Rafe's rarefied heights—a climb into the world arena that would have taken more than intelligence and a sense of humour to achieve. To get as far as he had he'd need uncompromising determination and a formidable ruthlessness.

In short, someone to be respected—and to avoid. Only too well did she understand the havoc a dominating man could cause.

The media lately had been full of him, from headlines about the signing of an important takeover to a photograph of him with a very beautiful woman in the gossip pages, but he'd soon be leaving Tewaka.

Hopefully to be away for another two months… That should give her time to stiffen her backbone and get over her disturbing awareness of the man.

* * *

When the meeting broke up—a little later than she expected—he caught up with her outside the library where the meeting had been held and asked, "Where's your car?"

Ignoring a suspicious warmth in the pit of her stomach, she indicated her elderly vehicle. "Right here. Goodnight." It was too abrupt, but she hid her expression by bending to open the door.

Their hands collided on the handle. The curbed strength Marisa sensed when his fingers closed momentarily over hers blitzed her with adrenalin. Before she could stop herself, she snatched her hand away as though she'd been stung.

And then it took every bit of composure she possessed to meet his focused, steel-sheened scrutiny without flinching.

Eyes narrowed, he pulled the door open and said coolly, "I rarely bite. Goodnight."

"Thank you." The words stumbled off her tongue and she hastily slid behind the wheel.

He closed the door on her and stood back.

Fingers shaking, she dumped her bag and the folder on the seat beside her and fumbled for the car keys. Why didn't he go away instead of standing on the pavement watching? Of course it took a while to find the key, but at last she finally stuffed it into the starter and turned.

Instead of the comforting purr of the engine, there was an ominous click, followed by an even more ominous silence.

CHAPTER THREE

"OH, NO." Swamped by a sickening feeling of impotence, Marisa jumped when the car door opened.

Rafe's voice, level and infuriatingly decisive, further fractured her composure. "Either your battery is flat or the starter motor's dead."

She fought an unnecessary panic, barely holding back the unladylike words that threatened to tumble out. Although she knew it to be useless, she couldn't stop herself from turning the key again, gritting her teeth when she was met with the same dead click.

"That's not going to help," Rafe told her, sounding almost amused. "It's the starter motor. If it had been the battery we'd have heard it try to fire."

Rebellion sparking a hot, barely contained resentment, she hauled the key out. It was all very well for him—*he* didn't have to worry about getting to and from work, or the cost of repairs. *He* could probably write out a cheque for whatever car he wanted, no matter how much it cost, and not even notice…

Rafe's voice broke into her tumbling, resentful thoughts. "This is an automatic, right?"

"Yes," she said numbly.

"So it's no use trying to push-start it. I'll ring someone to come and collect it and then I'll give you a lift home."

Marisa's lips parted, only for her to clamp them shut again before her protest made it out.

Wearing her one pair of high heels, it would take an hour—possibly longer—to walk back to the house. And she'd promised Tracey's mother the girl would be home at a reasonable time.

Then she had to get to work tomorrow. Marisa couldn't yet afford any help in the shop and week-end child care cost more than she could afford, so on Saturday mornings Keir came with her.

Rafe's voice brought her head up and indignantly she realised that while she'd been working through her options, Rafe had taken her assent for granted. He al-ready had his cell phone out and was talking as though to an old friend.

"Patrick? Can you come to the library and pick up a car? Starter motor's gone. No, not mine." Without look-ing, he gave the name and model of Marisa's elderly vehicle. "OK, thanks, see you soon."

He cut the connection and said to Marisa, "He'll be here in a few minutes so you'd better clear anything you want from the car. I'll take out your son's car seat."

Marisa scotched her first foolish urge to tell him she could do it. Frostily, she said, "Thank you", and groped for her bag.

She'd vowed she would never let another man run her life.

So did she wear some subliminal sign on her fore-head that said *Order me around—I'm good at obeying?*

Not any more.

Oh, lighten up, she told herself wryly as she got out. She was overreacting. Rafe was a local; he knew the right person to contact. Allowing him to organise this didn't put her in an inferior position.

But that clutch of cold foreboding, the dark taint of powerlessness, lingered through her while she waited.

Fortunately the mechanic arrived within minutes, a cheerful man around Rafe's age who clearly knew him well.

He checked the starter motor, nodded and said, "Yep, it's dead. We'll take it to the garage."

Surprised, Marisa watched Rafe help. He was an odd mixture—a sophisticated plutocrat on terms of friendship with a mechanic in a small town in New Zealand.

But what did she know of the man, really? He'd revealed impressive endurance and grim determination during their interminable trek through the Mariposan night and the rain. He'd made his mark in the cut-throat world of international business. Extremely popular with women, he'd been linked to some of the loveliest in the world.

It was oddly—dangerously—warming to see that he still held to his roots in this small town in the northern extremity of a small country on the edge of the world…

Once in Rafe's car and heading home, she broke what was developing into an uncomfortable silence. "Thank you very much for your help."

His sideways glance branded her face. "What's the matter?"

"Nothing," she said automatically, then tried for a smile. "Well, nothing except for major irritation at being let down by my car!"

Rafe asked, "How will you manage without it?"

"It won't be a problem." She hoped her briskness indicated her ability to deal with any situation. "As your friend Patrick seems fairly sure the car will be ready on Tuesday, I'll ring the taxi service when I get home and organise a pick-up for tomorrow and Monday."

It would be an added expense on top of the repairs, one she could ill afford, but she'd manage.

Rafe broke into her thoughts. "Can you drive with manual gears?"

Startled, she nodded. "Yes."

She'd learned to drive the tiny car her parents towed behind their house bus. And in Mariposa the only vehicle available to drive had been an ancient Jeep.

Although David had taken it out most days on to the estancia, and even when he didn't, the keys were never in evidence.

At first she'd believed he was concerned for her safety; Mariposan drivers could be pretty manic. Eventually she'd realised it was another way of exerting control.

Dismissing that bitter memory, she asked bluntly, "Why?"

"There's a spare car at home that might suit you." Rafe's tone was casual. Clearly he saw nothing odd in offering a replacement vehicle.

She gave him a startled look. The lights of an oncoming car revealed the austere framework of his face, a study in angles and planes. Even the curve of his mouth—disturbingly sexy with its full lower lip—didn't soften the overwhelming impression of force and power.

He looked exactly what he was—a ruler, born to authority…

A man to avoid. Yet every time she saw him—or thought of him—a forbidden, dangerous sensation darted through her. Fixing her eyes on the dark road ahead, she said firmly, "That's a kind offer, but it's not necessary."

"Think it over before you refuse. I know you open the shop tomorrow morning. Nine o'clock?"

"Yes."

"I'm coming into Tewaka just before then, so I could pick you up on the way. Then in the afternoon we could go out to my place and you can try the car."

"That's very kind of you…" she said warily, her voice trailing away as every instinct shouted a warning.

Dominant he might be, but it was ridiculous to think his offer meant he was trying to control her.

Ridiculous. Silently she said it again, with much more emphasis, while she searched for a valid reason to refuse.

"I can hear your *but* echoing around the car." The note of cool amusement in his voice brought colour to her skin. "Independence is a good thing, but reluctance to accept help is taking it a bit too far."

Crisply she returned, "Thank you, but there's no need for you to put yourself out at all."

His broad shoulders lifted in a negligent shrug. "If you're ready on time tomorrow morning, calling for you will add less than five minutes to my journey."

Marisa opened her mouth, but he cut in before she could speak, saying, "Small country towns—even tourist places like Tewaka—build strong communities where people can rely on each other when they need support. The car I'm offering used to belong to my grandmother. No one drives it now, but it's in good shape."

She rallied to say calmly, "I'll accept your lift tomorrow, but I really won't need to borrow a car. I can manage for a couple of days. And you don't even know if I'm a good driver."

Heat flared in the pit of her stomach when her eyes clashed with his sideways glance. There was altogether too much irony in the iron-grey depths—irony backed by a sensuous appreciation that appealed to some treacherous part of her.

She should be able to resist without even thinking about it.

Well, she *was* resisting—resisting like crazy.

Only she didn't want to.

And that was truly scary. Rafe Peveril was really bad news—danger wrapped in muscled elegance, in powerful grace, in unexpected kindness…

"How good *are* you?" he asked almost idly, his tone subtly challenging.

Marisa took a short, fortifying breath to steady her voice. "I think I'm a reasonably proficient driver, but everyone believes they're competent, don't they? It's very kind of you to offer the car—"

His mouth curved in a hard smile. "No more buts, please. And to set the record straight, I'm not particularly kind."

That made sense. Men who made it to the top of whatever field they entered usually didn't suffer from foolish generosity.

Remember that, she ordered the weak part of her that tempted her to—to what? Surrender? Accept being told what to do?

So stop that right now, she commanded abruptly, and squared her shoulders. She'd vowed never to allow herself to feel useless again and wasn't going to renege on that promise just because this formidable man was offering her the use of a car.

So she said, "If I needed the help I'd accept it with gratitude, but it's not necessary." She might not buy food for a couple of days, but the pantry held enough to tide them over and independence was worth it.

"Right." His tone changed, became brisk and businesslike as he turned the wheel to go up the short drive to the cottage. "However, the offer's still open."

Tracey met them at the door, her beam turning to blushing confusion when she saw who accompanied Marisa. Rafe knew how to deal with dazzled adolescents; his smile friendly, he offered the girl a ride back to the homestead.

Marisa watched the car go out of the gate and stood for a moment as another car came around the corner, slowed and then sped by. Shivering a little, she closed the door on the darkness, her thoughts tumbling and erratic.

Clearly Rafe Peveril was accustomed to getting his own way. And perhaps having grown up as son of the local big family, he felt some sort of feudal responsibility for the locals.

Well, he didn't need to. This new local was capable of looking after herself and her son.

She walked into Keir's room to check him. In the dim light of the hall lamp he looked angelic snuggled into the pillow, his face relaxed in sleep.

Her heart cramped. Whatever she did, she had to keep him safe.

But she stood watching him and wondered at the source of her unease. Rafe hadn't recognised her.

And even if he did remember who she was and where they'd met, would it matter so much…?

Pretending she'd never seen him before now seemed to be taking caution too far, her response based on a fear she thought she'd overcome. Thanks to the strength she'd developed, David was no longer a threat to her and no threat to Keir either.

But only while he still believed that lie…

She drew in a deep breath, wondering if the room was too hot. But Keir hadn't kicked off his bedclothes and a hand on his forehead revealed a normal temperature. Stooping, she dropped a light kiss on her son's cheek, waited as he stirred and half-smiled and then relapsed back into sleep, then left.

Back in her bedroom, she walked across to the dressing table and opened a drawer, looking down at a photo taken by her father a few days after she'd arrived back home. Reluctant even to touch it, she shivered again.

Never again, she swore with an intensity that reverberated through her. That pale wraith of a woman—hopeless, helpless—was gone for ever. Wiser and much stronger now, she'd allow no arrogant male to get close to her.

So although Rafe Peveril was gorgeous and exciting and far too sexy in a powerfully male way, she'd take care to avoid him.

She closed the drawer and turned away to get ready for bed. All she had to do was inform him she could deal with the situation and keep saying it until he got the message.

And avoid him as much she could.

But once she was in bed, thoughts of him kept intruding, until in the end she banished the disturbing effect he had on her by retracing the path that had turned her from a normal young woman to the wreck she'd been when she'd first seen him.

Loneliness, early pregnancy—and a husband who'd callously greeted that news by saying he didn't ever want children—had plunged her into a lethargy she couldn't shake off. A subsequent miscarriage had stripped her of any ability to cope. The shock of her mother's illness and David's flat refusal to let her go back to New Zealand had piled on more anguish than she could bear.

And then Rafe had arrived, tall and lithe and sinfully attractive, his intimidating authority somehow subtly diminishing David, and made his casual offer to take her home with him. By then she'd suspected she might be pregnant again and it was this, as well as her mother's illness, that had given her the courage to stand up to her husband.

Back in New Zealand and caring for her mother and a father whose grief-stricken bewilderment had rendered him almost helpless, she'd discovered that her pregnancy was a fact.

It had been another shock but a good one, giving her a glimpse of a future. With that responsibility to face, she'd contacted a counsellor.

Who'd told her not to be so harsh on herself. "A miscarriage, with the resultant grief and hormonal imbalance, can be traumatic enough to send some women into deep depression," she'd said firmly. "Stop blaming yourself. You needed help and you didn't get it. Now you're getting it and you'll be fine."

And during the years spent with her parents and looking after her son, she'd clawed her way back to the person she'd been before David. Her fierce determination to make sure Keir had everything he needed for a happy life had kept her going.

For him she had turned herself around. And because of him she would never marry again…

* * *

The next morning was busy, which was just as well. She'd been wound tightly, waiting for Rafe to call for her and Keir, but his pleasant aloofness almost convinced her that she had no reason to fear him. He might find her attractive, but a small-time shopkeeper was not his sort of woman. They tended to be tall and beautiful and well-connected, wear designer clothes and exquisite jewels, and be seen at the best parties all over the world.

In the afternoon she and Keir worked in the cottage garden; by the time she went to bed she was tired enough to fall asleep after only a few thoughts about Rafe Peveril.

She woke to Keir's call and a raw taint of smoke that brought her to her feet. Coughing, she shot into Keir's room and hauled him from bed, rushing him to the window and jerking back the bolt that held it in place.

Only to feel the old sash window resist her frantic upwards pressure. A jolt of visceral panic kicking her in the stomach, she struggled desperately, but it obstinately refused to move. Ignoring Keir's alarmed whimpers, she turned and grabbed the lamp from the table beside his bed, holding it high so she could smash one of the panes.

And then the window went up with a rush, hauled up by someone from outside.

Rafe, she realised on a great gulp of relief and wonder and fresh air.

He barked, "Keir, jump into my arms."

Gasping, her heart hammering in her ears, she thrust her son at him and turned, only to be stopped by another harsh command. "Get out, now! The verandah is already alight. The house will go any minute."

She scrambled over the sill and almost fell on to the grass beneath. A strong hand hauled her to her feet.

"Run," Rafe commanded and set off across the lawn and on to the drive, Keir safely held in his arms.

Half-sobbing, she watched as Keir was bundled into the back seat, then crawled in beside him as Rafe opened the driver's door and got in.

She had time only for a quick, hard hug before Rafe commanded abruptly, "Seat belts on. I need to get this car out of the way of the fire brigade."

So he must have called them. By the time Marisa had fastened the belts Rafe had the car purring quietly down the drive.

Rafe glanced briefly over his shoulder, his words cutting through the darkness. "All right?"

"Yes, thank you." Her voice sounded thin and wavery, and in spite of the warm summer night she was trying to stop herself from shivering in case it frightened Keir further.

"I've just come from the Tanners' place, so they'll still be up. I'll take you there."

Desperate to get Keir away from the sight of the burning building, she nodded. A few hundred metres down the road the fire engine tore past, siren wailing, lights flashing, followed by a stream of volunteers' cars.

Keir stared, fascinated. "Can we go back?" he asked eagerly. "I want to see them."

"No." She choked back a laugh that felt suspiciously like a sob. "The firemen need room to work and we'd only be in the way, darling."

"When I grow up," he told her importantly, "I'm going to be a fireman."

Her hand tightened around his. "When you grow up you can be anything you want to be."

The big car slowed, drew into the Tanners' gateway. All the house lights were on and Sandy Tanner came hurtling through the front door. He stopped, looked hard, then peered into the back as Rafe eased the car to a stop.

"Oh, thank God," he said hoarsely, wrenching the door open. "Come on, all of you, get into the house. Jo's got the kettle on."

Obeying, Keir and Marisa scrambled out and into the comfortable homestead, Keir with a wistful glance over his shoulder at the belt of trees that hid the cottage. "Our house is all smoky," he informed Jo Tanner, who gave him a swift hug.

"But you're here now and quite safe." She straightened and looked at Marisa.

Who asked steadily, "Could we put him down on a sofa somewhere under a blanket?"

"Of course we can. Come with me and we'll settle him."

Keir's hand clutched in hers, Marisa followed Jo into the big family room.

Briskly the older woman said, "You'll find the sleeping bags in that cupboard, with the sheets folded beside them. You'll want something else to wear too—I'll get Tracey's dressing gown. You and she are about the same size."

Still numb with shock, Marisa moved as if in a dream, spreading the sleeping bag on to the sofa and thanking the heavens that Keir still clutched his teddy bear. Like small boys the world over, Keir adored playing with his train and bulldozer, but Buster Bear went to sleep with him.

By the time Jo arrived with a summery, striped dressing gown she'd calmed Keir down enough to tuck him in and promise him she wouldn't go away. It was only when she pulled on Tracey's gown that she realised she was still wearing pyjamas.

OK, so the thin singlet top and boy-leg shorts would have revealed every line and curve of her body. Big deal, she thought trenchantly.

She had a lot more than that to worry about.

Everything she had was in the cottage, every precious memento—Keir's baby photographs, his wide grin showing his first tooth, her parents' wedding photo and the small silver-leaf brooch she'd loved to see her mother wear when she was a child…

Swallowing, she forced down the nausea that gripped her. She couldn't afford to break down. She had to be strong.

Nevertheless, when Keir dropped off to sleep, she had to force herself to get up and walk out of the room.

To her intense relief, the only person in the sitting room was Jo. She looked up and asked, "Has he dropped off?"

"Yes, it didn't take long. He rarely stirs, but I've left the door open and the light on just in case…"

Her voice trailed away and she blinked back stupid tears.

"He'll be fine," Jo said firmly. "Kids are surprisingly resilient. You're the one in shock, not him. I'll put the jug on—what would you like, tea or coffee?"

"It had better be coffee." She smiled weakly. "Jo, thanks so much—"

"Nonsense," Jo cut in firmly. "Don't worry, we've got everything organised. Rafe wanted you to go home with him, but I managed to convince him that Keir would be happier here for the night, where he knows us. The men are over at the cottage checking up, but they should be back soon, and then we'll know how badly the cottage has been damaged." She glanced at the clock and added more water to the electric jug.

Five minutes later a car pulled up outside. Nerves jumping, and acutely aware of the flimsiness of her clothes, Marisa leapt to her feet, bracing herself to meet Rafe's iron-grey gaze when he walked in. "What's happening? Is the cottage…?"

She couldn't finish, couldn't force herself to put it into words.

"Uninhabitable," Rafe said, not trying to soften it.

Marisa closed her eyes against his watchful scrutiny and dragged a painful breath into her lungs. "Did… Was it anything I'd done? I've been trying to work out whether I left anything on—the iron or…"

"Relax, it had nothing to do with you." Still in that level, dispassionate voice he went on, "It looks as though it was caused by someone flicking a cigarette butt out of a car window. The grass on the verge caught fire and the wind carried it up to the verandah. Once the balustrade caught it was pretty much all over."

"Was anything saved?"

This time Sandy answered, his voice sympathetic. "A good part of your stuff is all right, thanks to Rafe calling the brigade as soon as he saw the line of fire towards the house. The brigade killed the flames and Rafe and I helped them carry what was salvageable into the old garage there. It's smoke and water-stained, but it should be OK."

She dragged in a painful breath. "I'm so sorry, Sandy. Can you repair the place?"

"Not worth it," he told her bluntly. "It's an old house and once the fire got in it went up like a bomb. Bloody lucky Rafe happened to be passing and got you and young Keir out."

With an ironic smile Rafe said, "I had nothing to do with it, beyond yanking up the sash and catching the boy as Marisa pushed him through the window."

Foolishly, she wondered if meeting Rafe again had somehow set off some sort of tornado in her life, hurling all her careful plans into chaos…

She locked her fingers together to stop them shaking. Struggling to master her weakness, she blinked again, perilously close to collapsing into undignified tears as she recalled her frenzied terror when the window refused to open.

Rafe dropped one lean, strong hand over hers and squeezed. In a rock-steady voice he said, "Calm down. You saved yourself and your son, that's the most important thing right now. Everything else we can deal with."

We? Forget about that, she thought, and then felt surly, because he was being unexpectedly kind. "I haven't thanked you for opening the window," she said. "I was panicking, and Keir—"

He let her hand go and stepped back, waiting until she sank on to the sofa before continuing, "You were carrying something to break it—you'd have managed. Don't worry, Marisa, everything will be all right."

Conventional words, yet strangely they were of some comfort. When Rafe spoke in that coolly purposeful tone she couldn't imagine any power on earth gainsaying him.

Lifting her chin, she straightened her spine and asked with irony, "Is that a promise?"

Rafe smiled. "Only if you do as you're told."

And watched with interest as her delicate black

brows shot up at his blatant challenge. He was beginning to get some idea of her quality and admired that quick recovery and the strength it showed. Shocked and desperately worried, she was no weakling and her independence was bone-deep, as fierce and strong as the maternal devotion that had seen her get the boy out.

Sure enough she said sweetly, "I gave that up years ago."

He looked across at the two interested spectators and asked, "Jo, is that coffee I can smell?"

"Oh—yes, of course it is!" Jo went into the kitchen.

Rafe left half an hour later, farewelling Marisa with an order. "Make sure you've got the all clear from the fire brigade before you go over to the cottage."

"Yes, sir," Marisa said, clearly too tired to think of anything else. In her borrowed dressing gown she didn't look much older than its owner.

He regarded her with a lurking smile, a smile she returned. But before she turned away she said seriously, "Thanks, Rafe. You're right, I'd have got him out, but—I'm glad you arrived when you did."

Rafe almost managed to repress an image of her clad in pyjamas so closely fitting they revealed every curve of her delectable body and softly sheened skin. His heartrate had careered off the chart.

The memory brought his body to full attention, so much so that he knew it was time to leave. Laconically he said, "If you're going to thank anyone, thank Jo and Sandy. I'll see you tomorrow. Goodnight."

CHAPTER FOUR

MARISA's decision to get up early and go over to the cottage by herself was stymied when she didn't wake until almost nine in the morning.

Through the door, she could hear voices and laughter, and a glance at the sofa revealed nothing but an empty sleeping bag and Buster Bear. After an incredulous look at her watch she leapt off the inflatable mattress on the floor.

At the door she hesitated, then went back and put on Tracey's dressing gown. For some reason she had to brace herself before opening the door.

But Rafe wasn't in the big living area of the farmhouse. Relief and a strange loneliness hit her as she saw Jo and her daughter washing dishes.

Jo looked around and smiled. "Well, you look as though you've had a good night's sleep! Keir's out the front, playing with the boys. Tracey and I are just working out what clothes she can lend you until we get some of yours washed and ready to wear."

"Do you mind if it's jeans and T-shirts?" Tracey asked a little worriedly.

Marisa hesitated, then said with a wry smile, "Of course I don't mind. I'm just finding it a bit odd being a refugee. If it's all right with you, I'll wear them over to the cottage to see what I can find in the garage that Keir and I can wear straight away." A thought struck her. "What's Keir got on now?"

"I fished out some of the twins' old clothes and I put him in them. They're a bit too big but he doesn't seem to mind." Jo said firmly, "And you're not going over there until you've had some breakfast and a cup of tea or coffee, whichever you like."

"Thank you," Marisa said a little starkly. "You've been absolutely wonderful."

But Jo brushed her thanks away. "Tracey will bring some clothes along to the room you slept in and you can see if they're decent on you."

They were a little tight, but they would do until she managed to wash some of her own—always providing, she thought wearily as she walked along the road to the cottage, she had any left. Jo had offered to go with her, but she'd refused. She needed to be alone.

But the sight of the cottage stopped her, and for a horrifying moment she had to fight an urge to turn and run, snatch Keir up and run away from it all…

She dragged in a slow, painful breath and blinked back tears. Although the flame-blackened walls still stood, the whole place stank of smoke. Her heart clamped painfully when she saw the charred sticks of what had been hibiscus bushes against the verandah balustrade, their wonderful silken blooms gone for ever.

Some members of the fire team were back, checking the place and damping down any hot spots. She gave her eyes a quick surreptitious dab as the fire chief came out to meet her.

He said, "I wish we could have done more for you. Don't go anywhere near the house—it's not entirely safe yet. The garage is OK, though. You might like to go and check on things." He paused before saying a little diffidently, "We couldn't save all your boy's toys and only a few of his books."

Regaining control, she said, "Thank you so much. Some is better than nothing."

She'd find some tangible way to thank them, but right then she could only stand in the doorway of the garage, nostrils wrinkling at the stench of smoke, and fight for composure.

Someone had hauled out the drawers from the dressing table and dumped them and their contents on the floor, along with what looked like clothes from the wardrobes, Keir's toy box and a handful of his books. A few pots and pans had made it, but nothing much else from the kitchen.

The pathetic remnants of her life made her swallow hard, but mourning could come later. Right now she needed to be strong.

After a deep breath she walked in, only to flinch when the first thing she saw was the photograph on the ground—the one she loathed yet couldn't bring herself to throw away.

Unmarked by smoke and free from water damage, that pale wraith of a woman haunted her. Never again, she vowed silently, and snatched it up, only just stopping herself from furtively glancing over her shoulder.

"Are you all right?"

Rafe's voice—too close—brought her heart into her throat, blocking her breathing and setting her pulse rate soaring. Her fingers shook as she crumpled the betraying paper, the tiny sound it made echoing in her ears like a small, suspicious explosion.

Had he seen it—that betraying photograph?

In a thin voice she lied, “I’m fine, thank you.”

Don’t break down, she commanded, her composure cracking. *Don’t even think of it. You’ve coped with worse than this—you can deal with anything...*

Clearly he didn’t believe her, but he said only, “I brought some plastic sacks. Do you want me to help you?”

After a swift desperate struggle to subdue her rioting apprehension, she forced herself to turn, hoping her face didn’t show anything more than mild interest.

Rafe’s trademark vitality was as potent as ever and he examined her face in a searching survey that sent shivers the length of her spine.

All she could trust herself to say was a quiet, “That was thoughtful of you. Thank you.”

“It’s not the end of the world,” he said calmly and reached out his hand.

She stepped back, saw the infinitesimal narrowing of his eyes and said swiftly, harshly, “If you—anyone—touches me now I’ll start to cry.”

His mouth hardened. “Would that be so bad? It might be a good idea to release some emotion.”

“Later, perhaps,” she said bluntly, trying for a smile and failing badly. “There’s enough water around without me adding to it.”

Her breath huffed out in a long, silent sigh when he turned and walked out.

Like the lord of all creation, she thought ironically, watching the way the smoky sunlight kindled a lick of flame across his black head.

If he’d touched her she’d have crumbled, sagging into a humiliating heap of misery.

After another deep breath she hid the crushed photo in her handbag. She’d never be able to throw it away. It reminded her of how far she'd come and how strongly she refused to allow herself to revert.

So do something practical right now, she told herself, and after opening the big plastic sack, began to sort swiftly through the piles, grabbing the first clothes to hand. They stank of smoke and were damp, but a good wash would see them back in a wearable state.

Where could she go? At the most, she and Keir couldn't stay more than a couple of nights with the Tanners—it would be a total imposition after their kindness to her. So, even though she couldn't afford it, she'd have to book into a motel. Tewaka had several; at least one must have accommodation until she found somewhere more permanent.

Scarcely had the thought formed in her mind when she felt Rafe's presence behind her again and stood up, turning to face him.

He said, "All right?"

Jerkily she nodded.

He waited a moment, before saying calmly, "Where do you plan to stay?"

"I don't know yet," she said flatly, hating him for bringing her unspoken fears out into the open. Head held high, she tried to read his expression and failed.

Calmly he said, "Then I suggest you and young Keir move into my house until you find somewhere else to live."

Unable to believe he'd actually said what she'd heard, she stared at him, a swift rush of adrenalin surging through her.

One black brow climbed and his mouth quirked. "I'm pretty certain I haven't suddenly developed horns. It makes sense. Manuwai has enough bedrooms to billet a small army. If you think Keir needs reassurance at night, you could share the nursery suite, which has two bedrooms."

OK, so he didn't mean…what she thought he *might* have meant. Hot-cheeked yet relieved, Marisa recovered enough composure to say a little stiffly, "It's very kind of you, but I'm sure I can find somewhere—a motel, perhaps."

Amusement vanishing, he elaborated, "It's summer, this is a tourist area and the schools will be closing within weeks. Any chance of finding a motel unit—let alone a place to rent—is remote, possibly until the end of the holidays. Actually, you're not likely to get anything until after February because that's when people without schoolchildren take their holidays. I'm assuming you want a house within driving distance of Tewaka."

Numbly she nodded. "Yes."

Keir was very happy at school and she would *not* put him through the sort of upheaval she'd endured as a child. Nevertheless, the prospect of sharing a house with Rafe Peveril set every instinct jittering protectively.

Rafe went on, "Once summer is over you'll have a much better chance of finding a place."

His cool, reasonable tone grated her nerves. She blurted, "The end of summer is three months away."

The sound of her voice, sharp and almost accusing, stopped any further words. She drew a rapid breath and struggled for composure.

It took a lot of energy to steady herself and say with more than a hint of formality, "I'm grateful for the offer, but Keir and I can't possibly live in your house for that long."

"I knew there'd be a *but* in there somewhere," Rafe

said ironically. "So what will you do? Camp in the back of the shop?" He finished with a biting undernote, "Hardly a suitable place for a child."

Rallying, Marisa called on all her hard-won assurance to say briskly, "Please don't be offended. And, no, the shop is no solution. As my car appears to be unreliable, I'll see if I can find somewhere closer to town—preferably within walking distance—before I give you a definite answer."

There, that sounded sensible and practical and—her thoughts skidded to a noisy hum as Rafe nodded, a micro-flash of emotion in his eyes intensifying her unease.

"I'm not offended," he said coolly. "I'll ask around myself. Just don't be alarmed if nothing turns up." He gave a narrow smile. "And while you're looking around, the homestead is there. I'm heading overseas in a few days, so if me being there is a problem it needn't be."

The temptation to surrender to his calm assumption of authority was potent enough for her to pause before answering. Yet it fretted at something fragile and hard-won in her to accept Rafe's hospitality.

However, if she and Keir could find no other place to go, she'd grit her teeth and accept it for Keir's sake.

"I— No, of course it wouldn't be a problem. Thank you," she added lamely.

"Then I suggest you think seriously about it. Jo and Sandy will offer you beds, but it's not particularly convenient for them, or for you."

"No," she said swiftly. "I wouldn't dream of it..." Her voice trailed away as she desperately tried for some solution, only to realise she had no other options. That hard knot in her chest expanded, and she surrendered.

"Then—all right, I'll accept your very kind offer for a few days while I try to find a more permanent place."

Any place!

He didn't look pleased, merely nodded. "Fine. Thanks bore me, so let's have no more of them."

The urgent summons of her cell phone stopped him. She grabbed it and heard Tracey Tanner's agitated voice, and a background sound she recognised immediately. Keir—heartbroken.

"Can you come, please?" Tracey implored. "I've made him cry and he needs to see you're all right."

Marisa said, "We'll be there in a few moments", and switched off. Heading for Rafe's car, she told him over her shoulder what the girl had said.

At the Tanners' house a sobbing Keir ran into Marisa's arms and clung, while she looked her questions above his head.

Mrs Tanner frowned at her daughter. "I'm afraid he overheard Tracey talking to a friend about the fire and got it into his head that it was happening still, with you in danger."

Flushing, Tracey chimed in guiltily, "I'm really sorry—I should have checked to make sure he wasn't listening."

"Keir, it's all right. Stop crying now—Mummy's fine," Marisa soothed, aware of Rafe's hard face.

But his voice was cool, almost detached. "He'll get over it. Marisa is Keir's home base; now he knows she's safe he'll be fine. Won't you, Keir?"

Muffling his sobs in Marisa's breast, Keir nodded, but although he was manfully trying to control them, great half-choked sobs still shook his body.

Rafe went on, "And most of his toys are all right."

Acutely aware of an undercurrent of curiosity from the two Tanners, Marisa said briskly, "Keir, Mr Peveril helped me collect your clothes and your toys. What do you say to him?"

After a hiccup or two Keir emerged from her embrace to say, "Thank you. And my bulldozer?"

"Yes." Before he could run through a catalogue of his toys, she prompted, "And what do you say to Mr and Mrs Tanner and Tracy and the boys?"

Keir made his thanks, adding a codicil, "And thank you for the yummy chocolate, Tracey."

"Any time," Tracey said and ruffled his hair before exchanging a high five that dried the last of his tears and left him smiling. "See you later, alligator."

As they turned to go, Mrs Tanner asked in a worried voice, "Marisa, what are your plans? Is there anything I can do for you?"

Before Marisa had time to answer Rafe said smoothly, "She and Keir are free to stay at Manuwai until she finds somewhere else to live."

At Mrs Tanner's surprised look, Marisa inserted herself into the conversation. "Rafe has been very kind in offering us temporary refuge, but if you know of anyone who has a unit or a small place to rent, I'd be so grateful if you'd tell me."

"I'll ask around," Mrs Tanner said. She exchanged glances with Rafe and grimaced. "I'm afraid it won't be easy."

"Rafe's already warned me of that."

But the more people she had looking out for a place to rent, the more likely she was to find one. Tomorrow—no, as soon as they got to Manuwai—she'd call every estate agent in town to see if anything was available.

Once in the car Rafe glanced at Keir and said, "Straight home?"

Marisa nodded. "You took the words from my mouth. He's over-tired and overwrought. I'll do something about the rest of my stuff tomorrow."

Rafe nodded and started the engine and Marisa tried to relax, deliberately tightening and loosening muscles. It didn't seem to work. Every sense was alert and quivering, as though she felt an unknown danger.

In his car seat in the back, Keir was silent, but after several silent minutes he'd recovered enough to sing a song he'd learned at school, something about a car, only to stop halfway through with a cry that made her twist sharply.

"Look, Mummy! Camels!"

The car slowed and Marisa shook her head. "Not camels, although they're related. These are alpacas."

"Alpacas." He said the word with pleasure, then asked, "What does *related* mean?"

"Part of the same family," she said easily, aware of Rafe listening. "You're related to me."

"Like Nana and Poppa?"

"Yes."

"And like uncles and aunties like Tracey's Auntie Rose?"

"Just like that. Camels are cousins to alpacas."

While Keir digested this Rafe said, "They come from South America and they're bred for their wool."

From the back her son demanded, "Why don't I have any uncles or aunties or cousins, Mummy?"

Marisa said steadily, "Sometimes that happens in families, darling. The alpacas have wool that people use to make jerseys. I might go and see the people who own them to see if they make anything from them that we could sell in the shop."

As she'd hoped, that gave Keir something else to think about.

"Can I come too and pat the alpacas?" he asked.

"You can come, but they might not be tame enough to pat. Mr Peveril might know more about that than I do."

Rafe said, "I'm afraid I don't, but I can find out."

"No need," Marisa was quick to answer. "I'll do it."

Fortunately her words satisfied Keir and he settled back, humming to himself as he gazed out of the windows. Once more trying to relax, Marisa too looked out of the side window, her gaze skimming the hills and deep valleys of this part of Northland. On the very edge of her vision she could just discern a plume of smoke and had to swallow again.

Rafe asked, "Did you live in a city before you came here?"

Woodenly she answered, "Yes." Having to settle in one place had been a blow to her parents, but they'd needed to be close to the services available for her mother.

And she was being foolish to worry about the direction the conversation was taking. Rafe was merely making small talk, something to fill in the silence.

"In Auckland?"

"In the South Island," she said without elaboration. Right down in Invercargill, New Zealand's southernmost city, and about as far away from Auckland as you could get. Coolly she said, "I believe your property's on the coast."

Surely that was safe enough.

He inclined his head. "The house is almost on a beach."

An understatement, she realised when they arrived at Manuwai station. The homestead was a couple of kilometres from the road across paddocks that bore every sign of good farming. A thick, sheltering belt of kanuka trees separated the house from the working part of the station, the evocative, spicy perfume of their foliage permeating the warm air as the car moved into their shadow. From the feathery branches cicadas sent their high, shrill calls into the quivering sky.

A subtle, surprising delight filled Marisa and she leaned back in the seat. Ahead the drive bisected a large grassy paddock to head towards a far-from-modern house set in gardens that covered what seemed to be a peninsula.

She turned her head. Through the sheltering trees a basin-shaped inlet glittered blue against low, bush-clad cliffs. The point on which the homestead stood was its northern headland. In the opposite direction she glimpsed the long, silvery-pink sweep of a beach curving northwards.

"You're looking north to Ocean Beach and south to the cove," Rafe told her. "It's the only safe haven for about thirty miles and served as a refuge in bad weather for the scows that brought goods up and down the coast until the roads were developed."

"It's beautiful," Marisa responded inadequately.

A glitter caught her eye; she turned her head and glimpsed a helicopter parked just outside a hangar.

Well, *naturally*, she thought, mocking herself for her surprise. Of course Rafe Peveril would have a chopper on call. Did he fly the thing too?

Probably…

The big, orange-tiled house sprawled gracefully, its surrounding gardens melding imperceptibly into pohutukawa trees, their sombre foliage and twisted, heavy branches lightened by the silver reverse of each small leaf. Soon each ancient tree would glow scarlet and crimson and ruby, carpeting the beaches with brilliant blossoms like exploding Catherine wheels.

"This is the third house on the site—built in the 1920s," Rafe told her. "The family then had several very pretty daughters, so their father commissioned a house for entertaining. It's been modernised and added to down the years, but basically it's the same as it was then."

He spoke so matter-of-factly Marisa wondered if he took the house and its wonderful position for granted. A little wistfully, she tried to imagine what it must be like to know that your forefathers lived here, that for you there was always a base, a place you could call home…

The gates suited the mature opulence of the house, but were opened electronically, much to Keir's interest, and revealed a paved forecourt. Looking around, Marisa decided that the parking space was big enough to satisfy the social urges of a whole school of girls.

Rafe stopped outside the wide, welcoming front door and killed the engine. "You must both be hungry. I know I am."

"I am too," Keir piped up.

"I thought you probably would be," Rafe said, "so I phoned ahead to the housekeeper and warned her to have something ready that would please a boy." He lowered his voice. "And I wondered if you might like to go down to the beach afterwards."

But Keir's sharp ears picked up his words. Explosively

he said, "Yes, we do like to go to the beach!" and added, "Please, Mr Peveril, and thank you."

Tonelessly Marisa said, "That's very kind of you."

Rafe was too astute not to guess how she was feeling, but nothing of that knowledge showed in his face until they were out of the car and Keir had wandered a few steps away to gaze around.

Rafe looked quizzically down at her. "Sorry, I hadn't bargained for such good hearing on his part. It's been a while since I had anything to do with children. If today's not suitable, another day will be fine."

She tried for a casual smile. "We'd love to go to the beach today, wouldn't we, Keir?"

"Yes, please," he said with heartfelt fervour.

Rafe glanced at the opening door. "Ah, here's Nadine, who rules Manuwai with a rod of iron."

The housekeeper, a slim, brisk woman in her forties, smiled at both Marisa and Keir. "There's only one boss here and it isn't me. Lunch is ready if you'd like it now. I hope there are no allergies I should have taken into consideration."

"Not a one, thank you," Marisa told her. Keir enjoyed rude good health. She glanced down at him, sighed when she saw his hands and said ruefully, "But first we need to wash our hands."

CHAPTER FIVE

LUNCH was served in a sunny, pleasantly casual room where wide glass doors opened out on to a terrace overlooking lawns and the sea. Although Keir ate with his usual enthusiasm, his conversation revealed that his mind was bent on the beach rather than food.

After his second assertion that he wasn't hungry, Rafe pre-empted Marisa's response with a crisp, "We'll go to the beach when we've finished eating and after I've made a phone call, so it won't be for a little while yet."

Keir accepted this without protest. Uncomfortably—and not for the first time—Marisa wondered if she was depriving him of something vital by cutting his father out of his life.

Since her own father's death the previous year there had been no masculine influence on her son; watching him with Rafe now made her very conscious of Keir's simple pleasure in his presence.

As the years went by, that gap was likely to become a problem.

"Stop worrying," Rafe said.

Startled, she looked up, met a speculative gaze and felt her heart give a sudden leap. "I'm not," she told him, not quite truthfully.

"There's no need. Things will settle down."

His astuteness made her jumpy. It would be too easy to fall into the habit of relying on his strength.

On the way down a paved track to the curved stretch of sand at the base of the cliff, Rafe broke into her thoughts. "We've always called this the children's beach. It's very safe."

"And utterly beautiful." Mentally picturing the children who'd played here over the years, she looked around.

This exquisite boundary between land and sea—the brilliant sky, low red cliffs held together by the tenacious roots of the trees, salt and sand and the shrill calls of seabirds, a limitless ocean—this was the stuff of memories that made expatriate New Zealanders homesick.

And the unwavering self-sufficiency she sensed in Rafe, that deep inner confidence, was what she wanted—no, what she was *determined* to achieve for her son.

After some enthusiastic stamping and splashing in the tiny wavelets, Keir settled to build a large sandcastle, discussing the best way to construct it with Rafe in a very matey, man-to-man way that increased Marisa's tension.

If only there'd been an alternative to coming here. Not only was she far too aware of Rafe, but she didn't want Keir forming any sort of bond with him. Although he was surprisingly relaxed and easy with her son, there was no place for him in their lives.

And that was *not* maternal jealousy. As much as she could, she'd protect her child from any chance of future pain.

But she had to admit that Rafe was good with children. Possibly he'd had experience with them, although it didn't seem likely. What she'd read about him in the media indicated that most of the women who'd been linked to him were gorgeous creatures who flitted from party to party at all the "in" spots around the world. If any had children, no doubt nannies kept them well out of sight.

His world was very different from hers… Although Rafe might be attracted to her, she'd bet permanence was not his intention.

When he married he'd choose someone who'd fit into his world, not a nobody without a family.

Marriage? Stunned, she pushed the word away.

If—and it was an *if* so remote she couldn't ever see it happening—but if she ever again trusted a man sufficiently to consider marrying him, for Keir's sake any decision would have to be the right one, made with great care.

A decision that concentrated on good solid qualities rather than the impact of a glinting iron-grey gaze and seriously muscled elegance!

Rafe straightened up from a close examination of part of the sand fortification and glanced across to where she perched on a convenient rock. Her nerves tightened when he said something to Keir, who nodded and smiled and went back to his work as Rafe walked towards her.

Even in the casual shirt and trousers that had clearly been made for him, he looked like a model out of a photo shoot, one selling something magnificently masculine and expensive and powerful.

His first comment widened her eyes in shock.

"I gather Keir's father plays no part in his life."

Was he thinking of the mother who'd played no part in his?

"None," she said, her briefness making it clear she didn't want to discuss this.

His gaze narrowed slightly, but he nodded. "Or in yours."

"No."

After another level, penetrating look, he transferred his survey to the child. "Of the man's choice, or yours?"

Afraid to reveal too much of her nervous guilt, she monitored both her face and her tone. "Both."

"And you're happy with that?"

"Very." Her direct glance emphasised that he was trespassing.

But he was still watching Keir, his head turned to give her an excellent view of his profile. Her wary gaze skimmed arrogant nose and cheekbones and a jaw that epitomised formidable strength.

Handsome was too smooth a word to describe Rafe Peveril. *Commanding* sprang to mind, but even it didn't convey the essence of the man beside her.

It just didn't seem fair that any man should have everything. Except a mother, she reminded herself, and found herself hoping his stepmother had loved him.

Rafe turned his head, catching her eye. His gaze sharpened, darkened, ratcheting up her heart rate. "So is Keir the only man in your life?"

Very blunt. Why did he want to know?

Oh, don't be an idiot. You know the reason...

Her breath stopped in her throat. His open indication that he was as aware of her as she was of him fired a leaping, spontaneous excitement that took her by surprise.

Yet a cowardly impulse urged her to look him in

the eye and lie—or at least imply that she was in a relationship.

She couldn't do it. The lie that already involved him in her life without his knowledge still tasted bitter on her tongue.

And attraction—that heated, exciting tug at the senses, the disturbing, instinctive recognition of desire—meant very little. Perhaps Rafe was bored, looking for a diversion. He was free, and she was a novelty…

Whatever, he was dangerous.

"He's the only man in my life for the foreseeable future." Trying to ignore the odd husky note to the words, she added quickly, "He's heading for the water. I'll just go—"

"He's perfectly safe. Can he swim?"

"Not yet."

Rafe kept his gaze on the boy, the brilliant yellow plastic bucket Nadine had found clutched in his hand.

Marisa was being evasive. Her answers were straight enough and delivered with conviction, but a note of strain convinced him something was amiss.

He glanced at her. Face rigid, her posture tense, she was watching her son as though his life depended on it. Rafe felt a stab of compunction. She'd endured a gruelling twenty-four hours and he'd pushed her enough for the moment.

Quite apart from the possible mystery of her identity, she intrigued him. His initial flash of recognition had been accompanied by a primal, tantalisingly physical hunger, but that first mainly carnal awareness had been tempered by her stoic independence and her strength, and her love for the boy.

She'd come out to Manuwai only because she had no other option. He still didn't know how she felt about him—and that, he thought sardonically, made a rather refreshing change from most of the other women he met, who let him know they were very interested indeed, either in him, or his assets.

Crouching, Keir had proceeded to fill his bucket with sand. Rafe commented, "He's already worked out that wet sand holds its shape better than dry. He seems very grounded."

His shrewd gaze noted the silent, small signs of relaxation in Marisa before she said, "I hope so. He has his moments, of course, but he's mostly pretty placid."

"He doesn't mention any lack of a father?"

Tensing again, she kept her gaze fixed on her son and answered in a coolly dismissive voice, "Not so far, but I know it's inevitable."

"How do you plan to deal with it?"

Rafe watched her get gracefully to her feet, turning away to tuck the shirt into the borrowed, slightly tight trousers, and perhaps by accident giving him an excellent view of a swathe of taut, golden skin at her waist. Deep inside him a feral anticipation woke and refused to be leashed.

Dark lashes shuttered her green eyes and her voice was remote when she answered, "I don't know. I'm hoping it won't be for a while yet."

Her tone made it clear that was all she intended to say. And because he wasn't ready to take this any further right now he let her get away with it.

For the moment.

Always, he waited to move until he had every available scrap of information. The photograph he'd glimpsed in the garage had been enough to convince him she was Mary Brown.

What he needed to know was her reason for refusing to admit it.

The Mariposan agent's tone and words came back to him…*a few weeks after you and Mrs Brown left for New Zealand…*

In the hospital he'd been told they'd made it to a herder's hut, spent the night there and been found the next morning. He could—just—recall seeing the hut from the plane. After that there was a blank until he woke some days later in a hospital bed in the capital city.

How had they spent that lost night? Why had he never thought to ask? Because he had been too busy dealing with the mess that was the Mariposan agency, he decided mordantly.

He accepted that his cynicism had its roots in the knowledge that his mother had literally sold him to his father. It had been reinforced by the years he'd been a target for fortune-hunters. Was Marisa/Mary trying to set him up, and, if so, why?

You know, he thought sardonically, it would be for the usual reason—money.

She interrupted his thoughts, her gaze steady and unreadable. "I think Keir's been in the sun long enough." Her smile was set, her tone brisk and without emotion. "Besides, I need to wash the clothes I salvaged. We can't go on wearing the Tanner children's gear."

Rafe got to his feet. "Nadine will deal with them."

She glanced across at her son. Frowning, she pitched her voice too low for the boy to hear and said firmly, "Nadine is your housekeeper, not mine. I'm sure she's got enough to do looking after your lovely place without washing smoky clothes. I'll do it."

He said easily, "OK. Keir can stay here with me."

Brows lifting, she met his gaze, those cool green eyes unreadable, although her expression made it clear that he was, as his foster-sister would have told him, overstepping the mark.

"I wouldn't dream of it," she said cheerfully. "He doesn't know you well enough." She gave him a glimmering smile. "And I'm sure you've better things to do with your time than babysit."

He shrugged, matching irony with irony. "One of which is to make sure you try out my grandmother's car," he agreed smoothly.

She hesitated, then gave another smile, this one with wry but genuine humour. "OK, you win," she conceded. "But clothes first."

Keir's disappointment at being taken away from his construction work was plain, but he submitted with reasonably good grace to being brushed down and chatted cheerfully as they walked back up to the house.

As he'd expected, Nadine was instantly sympathetic. "Of course you'll want to deal with your own clothes. Just call out if you need any help."

Rafe said casually, "I'll bring in the sack." He looked at Keir. "Coming with me? You can help carry in the toys we found."

Keir was only too ready to go. Marisa said, "I'll come too. There are quite a few things to be brought in."

On the way out Rafe stopped outside a garage door and said, "You might as well check out that car now."

He opened the door and stood back to let Marisa look in, waiting with interest for her response.

After a moment of stunned silence, she laughed with genuine amusement. "*This* is your grandmother's car?"

"Indeed it is," he said drily, ignoring the swift stab of some unrecognisable emotion.

She sent him a flustered, half-accusing look. "I'd imagined a solid, sedate, *grandmotherly* car. This—" she indicated the sleek, low sports car in racing green "—is about as suitable for me as a motorbike would be. Keir's car seat won't fit into that tiny back seat, and where on earth would I put the groceries?"

"In the boot—it's very roomy," he told her laconically. "And if you look harder, you'll realise his car seat would fit."

After examining the space more closely, she gave a reluctant nod. "Well—yes, I suppose it would." She glanced down at her son who was inspecting the vehicle with absorbed fascination, then sent Rafe a straight, sparkling look. "It's gorgeous, but unfortunately it's just not suitable."

"How do you know? You haven't even sat in it," he pointed out. "It's in excellent condition—my grandmother used to drive very carefully, especially once she reached ninety."

"Kilometres or years?" she shot back, then stopped, a slight tinge of colour heating the skin above her cheekbones.

Rafe laughed. "Years. Keir and I will watch while you familiarise yourself with it."

Her reluctance was palpable, but after another long-lashed look at him she got in, her hands moving gracefully, confidently, over gear lever and wheel, checking the position of various instruments.

Hiding an odd impatience by talking to her son, Rafe waited. Finally she swung out, managing the exit with grace and style.

Smiling, her expression serene, she said, "It's a lovely

car and I wish I'd seen your grandmother in it. But it's really not necessary, and with the run of luck I'm having right now I'd be terrified I might drive it into a ditch. Thanks so much for offering it though."

Had she been composing that formal little speech while she sat in the car?

If his newfound need to know what really happened in those empty hours after the crash led him to a stone wall, he might feel slightly foolish, but at least he'd be free to find out whether the sensual promise of her fascinating eyes held true.

His silence brought Marisa's head up. A chill of foreboding ran through her when she met eyes of ice-grey.

That arctic survey heated when he smiled, a smile like an arrow to her heart, piercing and melting the armour she'd built around herself with such bleak determination.

That smile stayed with her, lodging in her brain like an alluring, far-too-dangerous irritant while she and Keir washed their clothes, hung them out in the fresh, flower-scented air and were shown into the nursery suite.

It was charming, with two bedrooms and a bathroom as well as a playroom that opened out on to a terrace and a garden. Closer inspection revealed that the garden was walled with timber slats and the only gate had a lock on it.

"Apparently I liked to explore," Rafe told her when he noticed her examining it. "The fence went up the day my mother found me down on the beach by myself." He glanced down at Keir, happily re-acquainting himself with his toys. "I was about half his age."

At her sharp breath he smiled without humour. "Exactly." He glanced at his watch. "I need to make a few calls but if you need anything, Nadine will help. I should be finished in an hour, so get settled in. You'll want Keir to eat when?"

"Six o'clock."

"Nadine can bring along a tray for him to eat here. When does he go to bed?"

"Seven o'clock." She knew she sounded abrupt, but a sudden wave of exhaustion was sweeping through her—not physical tiredness, more a soul-weariness that sapped her energy.

Too much had happened in too short a time; she felt her life slipping out of her control and didn't know how to regain it.

Rafe nodded. "Dinner is at seven-thirty. I'll come and collect you then."

She'd much rather have a tray on the small table in the nursery, but before she could say so, he continued coolly, "There's a monitor in the bedroom, so if he wakes or stirs someone will hear him."

After a slight pause she nodded. "Yes, fine. Th—" and stopped, warned by his sardonic expression to go no further with her thanks.

But over this at least she had some control. With her most dazzling smile she said, "I almost managed to hold back that time. I'll see you at seven-thirty."

Once he'd gone she stared around the room as though in a prison, before collecting herself. She couldn't crumple now. Yet Rafe's absence left behind an emptiness that startled her. He was…overwhelming, she thought, watching her son check out the bookshelf.

Idiot that she was, she'd not thought to bring his pathetic pile of books from the garage. Were his favourites a pile of ashes—the much-read tractor book and his favourite bedtime story about a cheeky dog, the bear tale she must have read a thousand times…?

Right then she could do nothing about them. And she didn't want to think of Rafe Peveril's disturbing impact, either. If his absence could make her feel this worrying emptiness, it was only because he was such a commanding presence, not because whenever she saw him her breath came faster and excitement sang through every cell.

Oh, she was fooling herself. His effect on her wasn't due to his height, nor the breadth of his shoulders or the lean strength that proclaimed his fitness. Or even to his harshly handsome face, its angles and bold features set off by a mouth hinting at a dynamic male sexuality.

It came from within the man, based on character and the formidable, concentrated self-discipline, along with his uncanny knack for reading the world's markets. Add a brilliant brain and he was a man to take very seriously.

She knew little about his rise to the top and not much more about his business empire, but she'd read an article in the business section of a newspaper praising his skilful governance for steering the organisation his father had left to its present prominence. The writer had also admired his firm control of it.

That had made her shiver. It still did. Control was something she understood only too well.

She banished him from her mind. "Keir, why don't you choose one of those books for me to read you later, then we can walk around the garden just to see what's there."

She had a son to settle in spite of a future that had developed a snarl of setbacks. Far better to bend her brain to ways of dealing with them, instead of mooning over a man who'd been surprisingly kind.

* * *

Although it took Keir a while to get off to sleep, Buster Bear eventually worked his nocturnal magic, allowing Marisa to scramble into the one respectable outfit she'd grabbed from the crumpled pile saved by the firemen.

It looked tragic—exactly what you'd expect from something rescued from a fire. Tomorrow night, when she had clean dry clothes, she'd feel more human.

But she bit her lip as she examined herself in the long mirror. What on earth was a woman expected to wear to dinner in the home of a mogul?

"Probably not a green fake-silk shirt and tan trousers," she informed her reflection, "but that's all you've got."

In spite of shaking them out and hanging them in the fresh sea-scented breeze from the window, their faint smoky aroma summoned alarming memories and not just of the previous night. Occasionally images of her sweaty terror as she dragged their luggage free of the plane wreckage still turned up in her dreams.

Squaring her shoulders, she turned away from the mirror and checked the baby monitor for the third time. Something too close to expectation fluttered in the pit of her stomach.

Of all the coincidences to be faced with, meeting Rafe had been the one she'd dreaded most—even more than seeing David again.

If this situation ever came to David's notice it would only add to Keir's safety. She couldn't—*wouldn't*—allow herself to regret the lie she'd flung at her husband when he'd demanded she return to Mariposa with him.

Marisa took a deep breath. She hadn't *cheated* Rafe—she'd just used his name and his reputation.

A knock on the door tightened every muscle, forcing her to take a couple of deep breaths before she opened it.

"Is he asleep?" Rafe asked.

Still stiff with tension, she nodded. "Yes."

Narrow-eyed, Rafe watched her close the door behind her. She looked tired, her exquisite skin paler than usual, those great eyes filled with shadows and mystery, and her lush mouth disciplined. Even so, erect and graceful, it was difficult to believe she was the woman he'd met in Mariposa.

So why didn't he challenge her directly, ask her what the hell this masquerade meant? He had no answer to that, because for once he preferred not to know.

He asked, "Did you have any problems settling him down?"

"Some," she admitted, "but I expected that, it's been quite a day. Buster Bear won in the end though." Her smile was slightly pinched, as though it was an effort. "He usually sleeps like a log, but I'm a bit concerned that he might have a nightmare."

"Does he have many?"

"Not many, but after hearing Tracey's account of the fire…" Her voice trailed away. She stiffened her shoulders and went on more briskly, "I'm glad there's a baby monitor."

Rafe opened the door into the small parlour. "Sit down and I'll pour you a drink. I remember you like white wine."

Would she realise that had been in Mariposa? She'd refused any of the red wine from the local wineries and her husband had said, "You'll have to excuse Mary—she only likes New Zealand sauvignon blanc."

And he'd given her some fruit concoction.

His words brought a faintly puzzled glance as she

accepted the glass, but he noted the fine tremor across the surface of the liquid.

Perhaps she did remember.

However her voice was light and without nuance. “Along with other wines. Perhaps you’re confusing me with someone else?”

So she wasn’t going to admit anything. He lifted his own glass, untouched until then. “Possibly. Here’s to a pleasant stay for both you and the boy.”

“Thank you.” She sipped, then glanced down at her wineglass. “Would it be possible for me to have some fruit juice too? I’m rather thirsty and I might drink this too quickly.”

A faint colour stained her cheekbones, but she met his eyes steadily.

Surprised by a swift impulse of protectiveness, Rafe told her, “A brandy would probably be the best thing for you, but perhaps not until you’re ready for bed.”

She gave a slight laugh. “Oh, I’ll sleep well enough without it. But juice would be perfect, if you have any.”

“Lime or orange?”

Not unexpectedly, she chose lime. At this time of the year juice from the oranges on his trees was almost cloyingly sweet.

He poured some for her and some for himself.

After a startled look at his glass, she said, “This is fresh, isn’t it? Do you grow limes here?”

“Along with other citrus trees. We have a large orchard that provides enough fruit for the other houses as well as the homestead. In the early days when fruit and vegetables had to be home-grown in isolated districts, my forebears made sure there was enough to keep everyone on the station going.”

“It was the same—” she stopped, an unidentifiable

emotion freezing her expression, and took another sip of the lime juice before continuing "—everywhere, really. I read about the early days on one of the high-country settlers in the Southern Alps—amazing that their wives managed."

She'd made a good recovery, but Rafe would have bet on it not being what she'd intended to say. She'd almost referred to Mariposa.

She walked across to the windows to gaze out into the warm summer garden. Gathering strength? It had been a beast of a day for her, and she'd almost given away the one thing she seemed determined to keep from him.

When she turned it was to say quietly, "This is delicious. Thank you so much for asking us to stay. We need to come to some arrangement about sharing costs."

Whatever he'd been expecting, it wasn't this. He returned brusquely, "I don't expect my guests to pay for any hospitality they receive."

Black lashes drooped over her cool green gaze, screening her thoughts. "Your guests are your friends. Of course they don't expect to pay you—and they can offer you hospitality in return. I can't do that." Her lashes came up and she met his eyes steadily. "Rafe, I don't need charity and I won't accept it."

"This is hospitality, not charity. Jo Tanner would have offered you a bed if I hadn't."

Her body stiffened and her voice was brisk and no-nonsense. "And I'd have paid my way there too if Keir and I couldn't find anywhere else."

Something in her tone told him she'd already spent some time trying to find alternative accommodation. "No luck?" he asked, almost amused by the sharp glance she gave him.

Shrugging, she said in a muted voice, "No luck at all. I didn't realise there were sailing championships this week at the yacht club, and I'd forgotten that next week the whole area has a country-music festival. Every bed-and-breakfast place I rang, every motel and hotel too, are booked out until well after the New Year."

Rafe said curtly, "Then forget about trying anything else—and forget about paying too." In his driest voice he added, "You may not realise this, but I can afford a couple of extra guests." When she looked up sharply he added, "Provided they don't eat too much, of course."

A wry, tantalising smile curved her mouth and quick laughter glimmered in the green depths of her eyes. "I'm not such a big eater," she returned, deadpan, "but Keir will probably amaze you with the amount he gets through."

"He looks as though he might grow into a big man." She'd know he was probing, even though he spoke in his most casual tone. "Is his father tall?"

After a taut moment of hesitation, she nodded. Rafe recalled David Brown—over six feet, and well-built—and felt an odd stab of something that was far too much like jealousy. Although he'd never expected virginity from his lovers, for some exasperating reason the thought of her making love to anyone roused an unsuspected resistance.

Experience told him she felt the same heated attraction he did. Which was possibly why she'd just tried to erect barriers with her suggestion of payment.

Setting boundaries on their relationship.

That stung. Periodically his sister accused him of being spoilt by too much feminine attention. Perhaps she was right, although Rafe hadn't been very old when he'd realised that many of the women who flirted with him were more attracted by his financial assets than his personality.

If he knew Marisa's reason for playing this odd game, he might find her reticence and refusal to cast lures in his path refreshing.

Impatience rode Rafe hard, knotting his gut. Once he had all the facts, he'd be better able to deal with the situation.

Her divorce from David Brown had been finalised just over two years after she'd left Mariposa. His PI had also discovered the boy's date of birth, almost exactly nine months after she'd got on to the plane for New Zealand.

Edgily aware of the saturnine cast to her host's expression, Marisa said, "You're going to get thanked in spades if we don't come to some arrangement about paying board. After all, I would have had to pay you for borrowing your grandmother's car."

"Borrowing doesn't require payment," he pointed out.

She stared at him, then summoned a lopsided smile. "It was a slip of the tongue."

"A Freudian one?" he enquired affably.

Her composure slipped a fraction. Heat warmed the skin across her cheekbones, but she kept her head up. "Freudian or not, it doesn't matter. I can't stay where I'm not allowed to pay my way."

He frowned, then lifted his broad shoulders in a dismissive gesture. "All right," he said crisply. "You'd better find out the going rate for board for one woman and a five-year-old child, plus the rental of a thirty-year-old car."

Suspicious, she stared at him and saw a gleam of amusement in the dense blue of his eyes. "I shall," she said stiffly. "And while Keir and I are staying here we'll keep out of your way as much as possible."

"Fortunately that won't be too difficult," he drawled and drained the rest of his glass. "The house is big enough for us to avoid each other quite successfully, but I expect to see you at dinner each night. Anything else—Keir's routine, for example—you'll have to organise with Nadine."

Privately Marisa considered the housekeeper had more than enough to do caring for this huge house without being bothered by the necessary changes a small child would make.

Staying here would only be a temporary measure. And Rafe was right. Not only was the homestead big enough for them to steer clear of each other, but by the time she left for work and came back again, the day would be gone.

Which left only the evenings…

Long evenings, as Keir was in bed by seven o'clock every night.

In spite of everything, the thought of dining each night with Rafe aroused a sneaky, unbidden sense of anticipation that startled her as much as it shamed her.

CHAPTER SIX

RAFE was a sophisticated, considerate host, making sure Marisa had what she wanted, talking about the district with the affection and insight of a resident, even making her laugh, yet his excellent manners didn't quite mask that subtle aloofness.

Until dinner was almost over, when he asked, "Is something wrong with your dessert?"

A note in his voice told her he knew very well that the poached pears and honey-flavoured crisp biscuits were utterly delicious.

Warning herself to control her expression more carefully, she said, "Absolutely nothing—Nadine is a superb cook. I was just thinking that once we've finished dinner I'll go and check Keir again. I don't want him to wake up in a strange place and not know where I am."

"Nadine would have let us know if he'd stirred. Eat up and we'll have coffee."

She said swiftly, "Would you mind if I didn't tonight? It's been quite a day…"

Rafe's mouth hardened, then relaxed. "Of course you can do what you want. As you say, it's been a difficult day for you." And he was perfectly polite when he escorted her to the nursery suite a few minutes later.

Yet every step she took beside him reinforced

Marisa's feeling of narrowly escaping something she didn't even recognise.

Tension had given her a slight headache. All she craved was a good night's sleep with no dreams about fire and no long, dark hours spent worrying over the future.

Keir of course was blissfully relaxed beneath the covers, with a parade of horse and unicorn posters looking down benignly from the walls. Smiling, Marisa picked up his bear and tucked it in beside him.

Keir was safe. That was all she cared about—all she could afford to care about.

As she always did, she bent and kissed his forehead, and as he always did he stirred and his mouth curved before he drifted off again.

Just as well someone was able to sleep, Marisa thought trenchantly some hours later, staring at the moon from her window. She felt like the only person left on earth. Usually a summer night brought some coolness with it, but not this one, and after discovering no night attire in the pile of clothes she'd scooped up from the garage, she'd gone to bed in a T-shirt and briefs.

Wryly she thought if she'd stripped off completely she might have stayed asleep instead of waking feeling sweaty and enervated. At least the air coming through the open windows was a little cooler than inside the room.

Breathing slowly, she gazed out into the night, a place of enchantment lit by the serene light of the moon. It was so still she could easily hear the soft whisper of wavelets on the sands of the children's beach and the long, lamenting cry of one of the waterbirds Waimanu was named for.

Where did Rafe sleep? Unbidden into her mind stole a picture of his lean, strong body sprawled out across a huge bed. Did he sleep naked? A sinful thrill warmed her. In Mariposa she'd been too exhausted and too worried to do more than accept his nakedness, but now she thought he'd be a brilliant lover…

On the other hand, why on earth should she imagine that just because he was a worldly success and had a very good body he'd be some—some super-Lothario?

Banishing the dangerous image, she left the curtains open, pulled off her T-shirt and went back to bed, where her plans for dealing with what had been saved from the fire were eventually overtaken by sleep.

An abrupt knock on the door brought her out of bed to race across the room, blinking sleep from her eyes.

Keir, she thought, panicking. She must have called his name, because through the door Rafe said urgently, "It's all right—he's fine."

"Then what—?" Marisa jerked the door open, then blinked again, staring at him in the glow of a dim light in the hall.

He'd obviously been in bed too, because all he was wearing was a pair of loose trousers, slung low on narrow hips. The soft hall light gilded bronze shoulders and he looked big and powerful and overwhelmingly masculine.

Marisa's pulse leapt into overdrive. After swallowing to ease a suddenly dry throat, she croaked, "What's going on?"

"I've just been rung by Sandy Tanner," he said, and grabbed her by the upper arms as she staggered. His voice harsh, he said, "It's not good news. The fire flared up again and burnt the garage down."

The words made sense, yet she couldn't process them. Dazedly she stared at him as he went on quietly, "With everything in it. By the time the brigade got back it was all gone."

It felt like a fatal blow to the heart. Every memory of her parents and every carefully preserved memento of Keir's life lost to her for ever…

Marisa sagged, but almost immediately tried to pull herself erect.

And then she was held in a strong embrace and Rafe said abruptly, "You don't have to take everything on the chin. You can allow yourself a tear or two."

"I c-can't…I can't…" she started to say, but got no further. Her eyes flooded.

When she choked on the next word Rafe said, "It's all right, I won't tell anyone," with a wryly amused note that finally broke through her resistance.

She couldn't stop weeping, not even when he picked her up and carried her back into the bedroom. Dimly she expected him to put her down and tried not to feel abandoned. Instead, he sat on the side of the bed and held her while she gave in to the tears she hadn't allowed herself since her father died.

Eventually it had to stop. She fought back the sobs and lifted her head, aware Rafe's broad shoulder was wet from her crying.

And that apart from a pair of briefs, she was naked, her breasts against his chest, one of his hands very close to them.

At a complete disadvantage, she muttered hoarsely, "I've got a handkerchief somewhere," and tried to pull away.

Rafe said, "I'll get some tissues from the box on the bedside table."

When he set her on to the side of the bed she shivered and hauled the sheet around her. His support had enfolded her, kept her safe and allowed her the luxury of grief—and threatened the life she was building for Keir.

She didn't dare let herself rely on any man—but oh, it had been immensely comforting to feel the steady driving beat of his heart against her cheek, his powerful arms shielding her from a world that seemed suddenly to have turned on her.

Comforting and—something else…

"Here," he said, handing her the box. He left her for the bathroom and came back shortly with a warm face flannel and a towel.

"I'm sorry," she whispered and hid her face in the warm, wet folds.

"Why are you sorry? For crying?" His voice was level and cool. "After the day you've had there'd have been something wrong with you if you hadn't released the tension somehow. And crying is a lot safer and better for you than getting drunk."

She shivered again and he said, "Where's your dressing gown?"

"Burnt by now," she said more steadily. "I'll have to call the insurance company. Again."

He sat down beside her and slung an arm around her shoulder in another sexless embrace. "Who are you insured with?"

She had to think; her mind seemed woolly and useless. When she told him he said, "Ah, yes, I know the local agent."

"I suppose you went to school with him." She moved away as far as the sheet would let, evading the too-confining weight of his arm about her shoulders.

Even in the darkness she could see the white gleam of his teeth as he smiled and got to his feet. In the dimness of the room he loomed like some primeval, godlike being. Every cell in her body quivered with delicious tension and she shivered with a sensuous, terrifying mixture of anticipation and apprehension.

It was the darkness, she thought wildly. If she turned on the bedside lamp everything would return to normal. Except that she was almost naked.

So what? It wasn't the first time she'd been almost naked in his arms. But he'd been unconscious then and they'd both slept heavily in the primitive comfort of their mutual warmth.

Now, standing so close to him, with the feel of his arms imprinted on her skin and the faint masculine scent still in her nostrils, she was seized by a sudden fierce longing for all the things she couldn't have—for support, for excitement, for love…

But most of all for Rafe.

Who had held her without the slightest sign of wanting her.

Keir, she thought desperately. Concentrate on Keir. And dealing with the fire.

"As it happens I didn't go to school with him," Rafe said, his voice amused, "but he's a decent chap and good at his job. I'll ring him tomorrow."

It would have been so easy to say thank you, to let him take over. He'd been kind when she needed it and she was grateful, but right now she had to fight this tantalising weakness that melted her bones and sapped her energy in a slow, smouldering heat.

"Thank you for offering, but I'll do it," she said unevenly.

He didn't object. "Will you be able to get back to sleep?"

What would he do if she said no?

"Yes," she blurted, so suddenly she made herself jump. "Goodnight, Rafe."

"Goodnight," he said, his voice level and uninflected.

She watched him walk out of the room, that reckless yearning she'd never felt before aching through her like sweet, debilitating poison.

Keir woke her the next morning, laughing as he tickled underneath her chin. She grabbed him and hauled him close for a kiss, then released his wriggling body to fling back the sheet and get up. The T-shirt she'd huddled into before she finally got off to sleep hung in loose folds.

And she remembered.

Remembered Rafe's arms around her, the powerful contours of his body against hers and the faint, subtle scent that was his alone—heat and virile male. Strange, but she'd always remembered it from the night after the crash, when she'd slept in his arms while rain hammered down on the grasslands…

Her skin burned and she said swiftly, "We have to get ready for work and school, darling." The previous night Rafe had told her he'd take her in and collect her and in the evening she could try out his grandmother's little car, and she'd agreed.

"Can we go to the beach?" Keir asked eagerly.

She glanced at her watch and blinked. "After work, perhaps."

The table on the terrace had been laid for breakfast and to her intense relief Rafe wasn't there.

"He's taking an overseas call," the housekeeper said

when Keir asked. She winked at Marisa and said, "I thought you might like to come and help me bring out the utensils, Keir." Keir's enthusiasm widened her smile. "If Mum agrees, of course."

Marisa laughed. "Of course I do. I'll come too."

"Stay where you are and enjoy the peace," Nadine advised. "Keir and I can do it."

I could get used to this, Marisa thought when they'd gone back inside, looking around at the garden and the trees, colourful and lush and beautiful.

And definitely not for her…

She bit her lip, forcing her mind away so she could concentrate on all she had to do. Get through the day first and then check to see what—if anything—could be salvaged in the burnt-out shed behind the cottage.

A shattering sense of futility gripped her, clouding her mind as she wrestled with a sense of obligation that was interrupted by a prickle of awareness between her shoulder blades.

After an uneasy moment she turned to look towards the house. Rafe was walking out through the French doors, moving towards her with the lithe silence she still found intimidating.

Colour burned up through her skin, accompanied by a pang of need so fierce it almost made her gasp. He looked at her keenly, but although her stomach knotted he didn't refer to her breakdown in his arms.

Instead, after greeting her, he said, "I've had news that will take me away from home for several days. I'll be leaving tomorrow afternoon, so after I've picked you up from work tonight we'll drop Keir off at the Tanners' and check out the garage at the cottage, then find out if you can drive the sports car."

* * *

"It's just like a toy car!" Bouncing with enthusiasm, Keir beamed at the sports car.

Rafe looked down at him. "It might look like a toy, but it's real enough," he said. "Let's strap your seat into the back and we'll see how your mother feels about driving us down to the road."

I'd feel a lot better if you weren't coming too. The moment the thought popped into her mind, Marisa looked guiltily away. He did seem to have a talent for reading her mind, but right then he was concentrating on getting the car seat into position according to Keir's instructions, delivered importantly and with pride.

She didn't want him to be so—so damned thoughtful. That afternoon he'd realised she was near breaking point when she'd seen the smouldering wreckage of the garage and he'd helped her control her shock and desolation by being coolly practical.

Nothing had been saved; the building and its contents were a twisted, blackened heap. Inwardly Marisa had wept at the loss. Yet after they'd collected Keir and driven home, in some odd, perverse way her grief had given way to a feeling of lightness, as though the fires had burned away the detritus of her past to allow her a freedom she'd never experienced before.

Wistfully, she watched Keir direct the attachment of his car seat, envying her son's confidence, his obvious enjoyment in helping Rafe. They could be father and son—both dark-haired and long-limbed…

Another thought to be firmly squelched. It brought with it an even heavier load of guilt.

"We're ready."

Rafe's voice startled her. She turned to see that the child seat had been fitted into the car and locked into place.

His smile was a little ironic. "Satisfied?"

"Yes." She looked down at her son. "In you get, young man."

He obeyed, but when she went to clip him in he said, "Mr Pev'ril can do it, Mum."

Something twisted in her heart. She said, "OK", and watched an amused Rafe follow more instructions, his hands deft and swift and sure as he slotted in the clip.

"There, that should do it," he said to her son's enthusiastic assent.

Marisa slid behind the wheel, fighting a difficult tangle of emotions. Love for her son mingled with fear that she was depriving him of a formative and necessary relationship by keeping him away from his father.

And then there was the confusing ache that had nothing to do with Keir.

She was so very aware of Rafe. Her body sang a rash, forbidden call whenever he was near, a call she didn't dare heed. If only he weren't so…well, so *nice* in his autocratic way. And Keir's pleasure in being with him was obvious from his confident, happy tone when he was chatting to Rafe.

Unfairly, she didn't want Rafe to be good with her son. Why wasn't he what she imagined a typical tycoon to be—dictatorial, overbearing and intolerant, puffed up with pride and a sense of privilege and entitlement?

Then she wouldn't feel this reckless attraction, this disturbing tangle of emotion and sensation that was changing from the initial strong, physical pull into something much more dangerous, an emotion with the power to change her life…

He lowered his long body into the front seat. Hastily she pretended to be studying the dials on the dashboard.

"Ready?" he asked.

Without looking at him, Marisa nodded and switched on the engine. "As ready as I'm likely to be. It's a good thing there's a long drive to practise on."

Although it had been some years since she'd used a manual gearbox, she soon remembered the technique as they set off slowly towards the road. From the back seat Keir chatted away, seeming not to mind that it was Rafe who answered his questions and pointed out various things he thought might interest her son.

At least concentrating on co-ordinating gear lever and clutch kept her from further obsessing about the man beside her.

And then they met the tractor. Not an ordinary tractor, but a behemoth, garish in colour and noisy.

"Stop here," Rafe ordered.

Marisa brought the car to a halt, smiling as she turned to look at her son when Rafe swung out of the car. Keir adored tractors and his attention was fixed on the vehicle and the man striding towards it.

After a brief discussion with the driver Rafe came back and bent to tell her, "The nearest gate is only about a hundred yards behind us, so back up and go into the paddock to let him past. Would you like me to do it?"

Powerfully tempted to surrender the wheel, Marisa set her jaw. Letting him take over would be a disintegrating reversion to the woman who'd allowed herself to become the wreck he'd seen at their first meeting.

In a clipped voice she said, "No, I'll be fine, thank you."

As though he'd expected her answer, he nodded. "Don't try to back through the gate. Reverse past it, then drive through. Once you're in the paddock you can turn around."

It wasn't exactly an order, but she had to conceal a bristling irritation as he straightened up again.

Go and talk to the tractor driver again, she urged silently.

Instead, he walked towards the gate, formidable and compelling, the sun gleaming red-black on his arrogant head.

A heady rush of adrenalin clamoured through Marisa, setting off tiny fires in every cell. Shocked by its force, she realised her hands were clammy on the wheel. As she dragged in a swift, shaky breath she ordered herself to be sensible, an injunction that did nothing to calm her twanging nerves.

Concentrate, she told herself fiercely. *Reversing is not one of your strongest skills, but for heaven's sake, this is dead flat and perfectly straight—you can do it. Just don't scrape the side of the car as you go through...*

How she hoped the mechanic would have her car fixed on Tuesday! And that she could find a place of her own soon—before Rafe returned from wherever he was going.

Tuning out Keir's chatter, she set the car in motion. Rafe stood beside the opened gate, watching her. Acutely conscious of him, she slowly reversed the car down the drive.

"I like Mr Pev'ril," Keir said from the back, waving at Rafe, who lifted his hand in response. "Do you like him, Mum?"

"Yes," she said colourlessly, because what else could she say?

Like? What a pallid, wishy-washy word. She didn't like Rafe Peveril—she wanted him.

There, she'd admitted it. *She wanted him.* Whenever he was nearby her treacherous body did its best to weaken her will. Even though every instinct whispered that he was a dangerous man with the power to cause her huge grief, she thrilled to the sight of him.

To Keir's enthusiastic commentary, she drove carefully into the paddock and turned the car to face the drive. The tractor thundered by, stopping a few metres beyond the gate and the driver swung down to speak to Rafe. Carefully she eased the car on to the drive again before stopping and glanced in the rear-vision mirror.

Something about Rafe's stance caught her attention. Whatever he was being told had made him angry. He spoke briefly and curtly, then strode towards the car.

"Here he comes!" Keir announced superfluously.

Marisa's hands clenched on the wheel. She took a huge breath and turned her head as Rafe got in, meeting eyes as cold and deadly as the moon.

Her stomach knotted and for a moment she froze in a familiar, dreaded fear. Whenever David had been angry with her he'd go silent, refusing to give her a reason and ignoring her tentative efforts to find out what she'd done wrong. Periodically he'd walked out, sometimes for days, leaving her alone without knowing where he was or whether he was ever coming back.

Involuntarily she asked, "Is something wrong?"

And stopped, angry with herself for reverting so rapidly. Rafe wasn't David and she was no longer a depressed girl rendered helpless by those long silences.

"Possibly." He paused, then continued in a level voice, "The driver's been clearing some gorse along the riverbank and noticed some suspicious plants on the other side."

"Suspicious pl—*oh*!" She stared at him. "Does that mean what I think it means?"

"Yes."

"On your property?"

"Yes." In a lethal tone that sent icy shivers down her spine, he finished deliberately, "Which could indicate that someone from Manuwai put them there."

Marisa blinked, then glanced in the rear-vision mirror. Clearly not listening, Keir had twisted around and was watching the tractor drive away.

She said, "They'd have to be awfully stupid, wouldn't they, because your workers would be the first suspects. Is the plot easily accessible from the sea?"

"In an inflatable it's reasonably easy to get at. And I don't for a moment think it's someone from the station. In fact, I have a pretty good idea who it might be."

Marisa switched on the engine and put the car in gear. Choosing her words with care, she said, "Let's remember there's a third party present."

Frowning, Rafe nodded and Marisa eased the car along the drive, asking, "So what are you going to do?"

"Call the authorities." His icy composure was far more intimidating than David's silences had ever been. "No one does that on my land and gets away with it."

CHAPTER SEVEN

BACK at Manuwai Marisa parked the car carefully in the garage and held out the keys.

"Keep them," Rafe told her negligently. "Use this car until you've got your own back."

"I… Thank you." It was on the tip of her tongue to ask when he'd be returning from his trip, but she restrained herself in time. It would have sounded far too personal—as though she had some right to know.

He said to Keir, "Look after your mum while I'm away, young man. She's had a tough day."

Keir managed the difficult task of registering both pride and dismay. "Yes, but when are you coming home?" he asked.

"Probably after six more sleeps."

Watching Keir struggle with disappointment, Marisa winced. It was one thing to wonder if her son needed more male influence in his life; that he was fast fixing on Rafe as that influence was something else entirely. She didn't want Keir to become attached to him, only to find he had no place in Rafe's life.

She fought back a tide of weariness and put Keir to bed, where he dropped off immediately.

When she found that Nadine had ironed their smoke-stained clothes, weak tears sprang to her eyes as she stammered thanks.

"You're worn out and no wonder," Nadine said briskly. "I'll make you a cup of tea."

Marisa straightened. "I'd love that, but I need a shower more, and then shall we sit down and work out a system? I know our being here is making extra work for you, but I'll make sure it's as little as possible."

The housekeeper smiled. "I enjoy having people around and it's lovely to have a child in the house again. Makes it a home, somehow."

Which warmed Marisa, but once she'd drunk the cup of tea she rang around the various estate agents.

And got the same answer—nothing to rent.

Still she kept trying, spurred on every morning by Keir's eager query, "Is Mr Peveril coming home today?" Rafe had departed in the chopper, which he *did* fly to and from the local airport, to Keir's complete entrancement, but every morning when either Marisa or Nadine said, "No, not today," his face fell.

Marisa understood his feelings. Lovely as Manuwai homestead was, the place seemed empty without its driving force, the man who owned it.

She missed Rafe like an ache for something she'd never attain, a hunger that could never be satisfied.

Yet it was too easy to settle, to relax, to let the big house embrace them. She and Nadine worked out their system and enjoyed each other's company, she met several of the farm workers, and Keir demanded to be allowed to travel in the school bus with his new best friend, the son of one couple.

"No, darling, we can't do that," she said at first.

Thrusting out his lower lip, he produced something

too close to a whine. "Why? Manu said his mum said it was all right and she'd take me with him when she takes him and the other kids on the bus down to the gate."

She thought for a moment. "Here's what we could do. I'll talk to Manu's mother and if she's happy to take you down you could go in the morning, but after school Nadine is too busy to look after you. And it's not her job. So in the afternoon you'd still have to go to the day-care centre and the shop."

He wavered, then gave a reluctant nod.

Manu's mother laughed when she rang. "I've been waiting for your call," she said cheerfully. "My little scamp told me all about this plan he and Keir dreamed up. Of course I'll pick Keir up in the mornings—it'll be no bother."

So the next morning Marisa watched Keir climb into Ngaire Sinclair's car, feeling rather as she had on his first day at school.

On the third day Patrick the mechanic rang to say her own car was fixed.

"But it's going to need more work done soon," he warned her when she arrived to pick it up.

Anxiously Marisa asked, "Expensive work?"

He grimaced. "Yeah, 'fraid so. Rafe told me to give it a good going-over so I took it for a drive and your transmission's slipping."

"What does that mean?"

He answered soberly, "Basically it means you'll be driving it one day and it'll stop. And then it will cost you."

Marisa drew a deep, impeded breath and drove carefully home, anxiously trying to work out how she could afford to pay for any future repairs. Renewed efforts to find somewhere to live close to town still met without success. That and dealing with her insurance claim kept her busy, and the Christmas buying frenzy was slowly starting.

A week after Rafe had left, she tucked Keir into bed, then walked along to the small parlour where she'd joined Rafe that first night. She pushed open the door and took two steps inside before she realised she wasn't alone. Her heart stopped, then began thudding in an irregular tattoo as an incredulous, terrifying delight filled her.

"How— I didn't hear the chopper," she said a little indignantly.

"I came out by car."

Rafe felt a swift jab of something too close to compunction. She looked tired, and although her face was impassive, she held herself stiffly, as though ready to stand her ground and fight.

At their first meeting in Tewaka he'd recognised the brittleness beneath the bright confidence, but now—now he knew exactly what caused it.

He should despise her. He did despise her, yet whenever he saw her his body sprang to life, reacting with hot, sexually charged arousal…

Marisa met his gaze with what could almost have been defiance, but her voice was unsteady as she went on, "You're back early."

"I've done what I had to do." He poured a glass of wine and held it out to her. "You seem startled."

Her smile looked genuine, but no amusement showed in her eyes and again he sensed that tight control.

"Thank you," she said and sipped an infinitesimal amount, red lips curved against the glass. "Not startled, just a bit surprised. I didn't think Nadine was expecting you for another couple of days."

The sensation in his gut expanded into lust, like an arrow from some malicious god. *Not now*, he thought grimly, silently cursing his unruly body.

His voice sounded harsh when he said, "Nadine expects me when she sees me."

After another fleeting glance, she hurried into speech. "I've called social services, so I know how much I should be paying you for board." Her voice was almost challenging as she gave him a figure.

Rafe nodded. The amount meant nothing—he'd already decided to put the money into a bank account for her son. But her immediate mention of it meant she was still trying to set barriers between them, reduce everything to a commercial basis.

And if he was going to see this thing through, he needed to follow her example and ignore the fact that the pulsating awareness between them was not only mutual, but unlike anything he'd ever experienced before. The situation was too complex, muddied by other considerations, other concerns.

They had a lot more to deal with than this unforeseen and extremely disruptive physical reaction.

Although, he thought ironically, it could work in his favour…

And cursed again at the leap of hunger in his blood.

As though she sensed it Marisa took a step back and said jerkily, "What a lovely, serene room this is."

"It was my mother's favourite," he told her. "I think the women of the house have always used it for their refuge."

She seemed to be interested. "It must be very…" she stopped a moment or two, finally producing with a slight grimace "...*grounding*, I suppose is the word I'm looking for—to grow up in a house where your family has lived for generations. Unusual too in New Zealand."

"Not so very unusual—plenty of families still live where their ancestors settled. There have been three houses here, actually. My several-times-great-grandfather and his wife camped in a canvas tent until the local tribe showed them how to make a more permanent structure—a *whare* with a frame of manuka poles thatched with the fronds of nikau palms."

He noticed her face go rigid for a fleeting moment, then the long lashes swept down. When they came up again the green eyes were blank and shallow as glass.

So many damned secrets. Why? And the need to know every last one of them was becoming intolerable.

But her words surprised him. "His wife must have been so lonely here."

"You'd think so, but it wasn't long before she had children to look after, and she was an ardent gardener."

"I suppose she had to be."

He nodded. "She became friends with quite a few of the women of the tribe here. In fact, her oldest son—who took over Manuwai when his father died young—eloped to Australia with the daughter of the chief. She was a great beauty."

Her eyes widened. "Goodness, what happened?"

"The girl's parents were furious," he told her drily. "She'd been promised to a chief from the Waikato region so it caused quite a scandal. But once the babies started to arrive all was forgiven."

Marisa stiffened again, but forced herself to relax. "That usually happens, doesn't it?" she said neutrally. "Children have a habit of winding their way into people's hearts."

Although his gaze was far too keen for comfort, his voice was casual. "Where did you grow up?"

For a second she hesitated, then said smoothly and quickly, "Everywhere."

At his raised brows, she managed to produce a smile. "Quite literally. My parents were gypsies—not real ones, but they travelled all over the country."

"In a caravan?"

"No, a house bus."

"An interesting childhood," he observed noncommittally, his gaze never leaving her face.

It was like being targeted by lasers. Shrugging, Marisa said, "I'm afraid I didn't appreciate it as I probably should have. I wanted to be like other kids and stay in one place."

"Why?"

"Herd instinct, I suppose." Before he could put any more questions she asked, "Did you ever hanker for a different life?"

"There was enough here to keep me happily occupied while I was at primary school. But I spent my secondary years away at boarding school and by the time I left I knew I didn't want to come back here and farm the place as most Peverils before me had. So I went to university and did a couple of degrees before setting off to make my fortune."

There had been problems about that decision, she deduced from the raw undernote to his words.

Rafe went on in a coolly judicious tone, "But Waimanu has always been my home, so your choice of word was apt. Grounded is exactly how the place makes me feel. What did your parents do to earn a living?"

"My mother was a fantastic knitter and embroiderer, and my dad made gorgeous wooden toys. Between them they earned enough for us to keep travelling. They loved the life."

So much that she wondered if the illness that forced her mother to stay in one place had worn away their will to live.

She scotched that thought with a rapid, twisted smile. "I'm afraid I was born without their wanderlust, or their manual skills."

"You can paint," he said crisply. "Gina is a connoisseur and she rates your oil very highly."

His words surprised and warmed her. "I have a small talent, that's all. I'm delighted she likes the picture, but I hope she's not expecting it to increase in value much over the years."

Painting was another thing she'd had to surrender in the mockery that had been her marriage. David had considered it a frivolous waste of time. At first she'd thought he didn't understand the pleasure she got from it, but soon she'd realised he understood too well—he saw it as competition, something that took her attention away from him. Without making a decision to give it up, she'd found it impossible to keep going when somehow her materials had disappeared and new ones never arrived.

Bad memories. She dismissed them and sipped some more wine, trying to think of a way to steer the conversation back to Rafe.

"Perhaps you don't fully appreciate the talents that were developed through your unconventional life with your parents. And surely growing up in that sort of milieu must have given you the knowledge and the skills to choose your stock when you set up the shop?"

Marisa gave him a swift, surprised look. "I suppose it did," she said quietly. "Tell me, how big is Manuwai?"

The acreage he gave startled her. "That's huge," she said involuntarily.

He shrugged. "We don't give up what's ours," he said.

A note in his voice sent an involuntary shiver through her.

He went on, "Have you worked out a schedule with Nadine?"

Marisa's smile probably showed too many teeth. Or perhaps it was the saccharine sweetness of her tone when she said, "Yes, sir", that hardened his gaze.

"Did that sound like an order?"

"Very much," she told him coolly.

His smile was a little taunting. "And you don't respond well to them?"

"I tend not to respond to orders at all."

She hoped her voice was a lot more confident than she felt. Periodically the old Mary Brown emerged from beneath the carefully confident shell she'd built around herself, but no one was ever going to control her again.

Not even a man whose efficiency in running a worldwide organisation earned him general respect and admiration.

"Indeed, why should you?" he said negligently. "However, I didn't intend to bark out commands."

Marisa shrugged. "As it happens, Nadine and I work very well together."

"Good," he said, but absently as he checked his watch. "And if we're to avoid her sternest face, we'd better get ourselves to the table. It's such a pleasant evening we're eating out on the terrace."

Once outside, he said, "I assume Keir's already asleep."

"Well and truly. They had swimming sports at school today."

"How did he do?"

"He told me he came third in the dog paddle. That was clearly a big deal." She smiled a little at the memory of his innocent delight. "He informed me that next year he's going to win."

"You didn't go?"

"No. I had to look after the shop."

He gave her a keen glance but made no comment, possibly guessing that she'd spent quite a bit of the two hours allotted to the sports wishing she could be there.

She said sturdily, "And thanks very much for the loan of your grandmother's car. It's been fun driving it. Your friend Patrick told me that you'd asked him to give my car a good going-over."

"Did he?" He looked amused.

She wanted to tell him to step back from her, keep out of her business, but it seemed churlish. "Thank you," she said woodenly, and looked around. "How lovely it is out here."

The terrace garden always reminded Marisa of photographs she'd seen of tropical resorts, usually in glossy magazines filled with impossibly beautiful people. But tonight everything seemed brighter, more sweetly scented, more—well, just *more.*

Because Rafe was here…

After sitting down she kept her gaze fixed on the circle of lawn bordered by plants with dramatic leaves and bold flowers.

"The light's not too bright?" Rafe asked.

"Not a bit." A canopy sheltered them as the sun sank towards the west and a little breeze sighed past, carrying the fresh, green scent of foliage and flowers, the tang of salt.

Some people, Marisa thought almost enviously, had all the luck.

No, luck was for lottery winners. Rafe's life might be based on the hard work of the generations who'd lived at Waimanu before him, but his own efforts had propelled him further than they had gone.

And he was an excellent host. Over the meal she engaged in a spirited discussion that had her forgetting—almost—her very equivocal situation.

What she couldn't ignore was the swift build of excitement, the intoxication of exchanging views with a man whose incisive brain stimulated hers—and the more subtle stimulation of green eyes meeting grey, the deep timbre of his voice, the way a stray sunbeam lingered across his head, kindling a red-black flame before dying as the sun went down and twilight descended upon them.

He was dynamite, his potent masculinity adding to the impact of his powerful personality.

"Don't you like that wine?" Rafe asked.

"It's lovely, but I've had enough, thank you," she said swiftly.

She didn't need wine. This rare excitement that throbbed through her, exhilarating and heady, came from her heart's response to the man who watched her across the table.

He leaned back in his chair and looked at her, his gaze intent yet oddly chilling. Without preamble, he said in a voice that held no expression at all, "I've just flown back from Mariposa."

Her heart stopped. Literally.

Then it started up again, hammering so loudly she couldn't hear the silken song of the waves as they kissed the beach. She felt the colour drain from her skin, leaving it cold and taut. For a horrifying moment she thought she might faint.

Not now, she thought frantically, her gaze locked on to the cold grey of his. She dragged in a deep breath and forced her spinning, shocked brain into action.

"How interesting," she finally got out.

And closed her mouth against any further words in case her voice broke and she shattered with it into a million pieces.

He didn't move. "Is that all you have to say?"

Her skin tightened in a primitive urge to flee, to grab Keir and run as though the hounds of hell were after them. She resisted the urge to swallow and managed to speak. "What do you think I should say?"

"You might start," he said, his tone so level it sounded like a judge's delivery of a verdict, "by telling me exactly who fathered your son."

CHAPTER EIGHT

MARISA dragged a shaky breath into airless lungs. Silence stretched between them as she desperately searched for something—anything—to say. Her voice sounded limp and strained when she finally said, "I have no idea what business that is of yours. Why do you ask me?"

Rafe was still leaning back in his chair, watching her like a predator about to strike the killing blow. "In Mariposa I discovered that when we were found after the crash both of us were in bed together. Naked." His gaze narrowed into iron-hard intimidation. "Did we make love?"

Colour flooded her skin. "No!"

Too late she realised her explosive denial had betrayed her identity. Dismay and a kind of fear paralysed her.

Not a muscle moved in Rafe's hard, handsome face. Without apparent interest he asked, "So why were we naked?"

Abandoning hope of keeping up the pretence, she summoned every ounce of willpower to keep her voice steady. "You were naked—I was not. We crashed in a rainstorm. By the time we reached the hut we were both drenched and you—you looked like death. You were shivering, and I couldn't—"

Marisa stopped, recalling her helpless terror as she'd tried to work out what to do.

"Go on," he said tonelessly.

She bit her lip, then forced herself to continue in a flat voice. "There was a sort of bed—a hammock, really, made of cowhide nailed to a wooden frame. At first I thought we could use the frame to make a fire, but there were no matches. It was freezing…" She took another breath and finished rapidly, "And the only covering was another cowhide. It had no warmth to it. So I went back to the plane and retrieved our luggage."

He said quietly, "In the rain?"

"It hadn't stopped." Terrified the plane might somehow explode, and ashamed of her primitive, anguished fear of the dead pilot, two things had kept her going—fear Rafe might die if she couldn't warm him and the need to collect her passport, her only hope of freedom.

By the time she returned to the hut she was so tired she'd ached as though she'd been beaten, but worse than her exhaustion was seeing Rafe collapsed on the sorry excuse for a bed, his indomitable will finally conquered by the injury.

For a shattering moment she'd thought he was dead.

All emotion drained from her voice she went on, "When I got back I had to shake you awake, but I could tell you had no idea what was happening. I managed to persuade you out of your wet clothes, but after that you relapsed into unconsciousness again, so I couldn't get you into anything dry."

Not that their clothes had been dry exactly, but damp had been an improvement on sodden.

Something of the cold dismay that had overtaken

her then swept through her now. She steadied her voice and said, "I took all the clothes from both our cases and spread them over you and put the skin over them, but you didn't stop shivering. You were cold—so cold—and I thought you might die before anyone came."

Nothing showed in his face, nothing but harsh control. "And you?"

She stared at him.

He said crisply, "I assume you were wet too, and just as exhausted."

Surprised, she said, "I hadn't been hurt. You probably don't remember, but you pushed my head down just before impact and all I got were a few bruises. I was soaked and cold, so I stripped off everything except my bra and pants and got in beside you and held you, and after a while we both warmed up and went to sleep."

His arms had closed around her as though he was accustomed to holding a woman in his bed. That firm, confident embrace had somehow reassured her that he'd survive until rescuers arrived.

"And that's how they found us," he said, but not as though it were any revelation.

His steady, remorseless gaze searched her face. Marisa forced herself to master her chaotic emotions and the choppy, disconnected thoughts racing through her mind.

"The noise of the chopper woke me. I managed to haul on some clothes, but you…you couldn't." He'd been breathing and he was warm, but that time she hadn't been able to wake him.

"In Mariposa," he said, his voice deliberate, "the general opinion is that we made love."

Head held high, Marisa met his unreadable scrutiny

with a steady one of her own. "We didn't," she said bluntly. "Neither of us was in any fit state, believe me."

"So why does your husband believe I am Keir's father?"

Oh, God, how did he know that? She closed her eyes, then forced them open again to meet his coldly implacable gaze. Tension knotted her nerves, scraped her voice raw, but she owed him an explanation. "Because I told him you were. It was a lie."

Still his expression didn't change, and now—too late—she understood the hard power of the man. The ruthless determination that had got him out of that plane and supported him to the hut was as much a part of him as his brilliance and the splendid bone structure of his face.

Still in that cold, uncompromising tone he asked, "Why?"

Her throat was dry. This must be how a person on trial felt. "Because it was the only thing I could think of that would keep my child safe."

"What do you mean—safe?" The question came hard and fast as he straightened. "Did he beat you?"

She shook her head. "He never hit me." And couldn't say anything more.

Because in spite of David's rigid self-control, the threat of his leashed violence had been ever present, eventually dominating her life. Strangely, Rafe's anger didn't frighten her; he was truly formidable, but she couldn't imagine him ever losing that iron discipline.

Not even now, when he had every reason to be both disgusted and furious.

An inner caution taunted her, *How do you know that? How can you be so sure?*

She'd been so wrong before—could she be equally wrong about Rafe?

His regard for her and Keir had almost convinced her that he had no taint of her ex-husband's desire to control. Yet it could be because he'd wondered if Keir might be his own…

Rafe stayed silent, waiting. She took a deep breath and tried to explain. "David wants—*needs* to control. I think it must be a compulsion. That's why he took the job in Mariposa, away from everyone we knew. The people there were lovely—so hospitable—but David wouldn't join in the district's social life. And he didn't want me to, either."

"You can drive," Rafe said, frowning. "What stopped you from going out on your own?"

"We didn't have a car."

His brows rose. "There was one on the estancia—a Jeep."

"It was usually needed—David took it with him."

Rafe's frown deepened. "And when it wasn't?"

She flushed, angry with herself for being so embarrassed after all this time. "When he didn't need it he read the odometer before he left the house and again after he came home." Once, early on and feeling mutinous, she'd driven into the nearest town, a mere village, but the resultant inquisition had been such a fraught experience she'd never repeated it.

She glanced at Rafe's hard face and said flatly, "It happened. It will *never* happen to me again."

"You're implying that he kept you a prisoner on the estancia."

"Yes," she said, unsurprised by his attitude.

Rafe said, "The contrast between you now, and the

woman I saw in Mariposa, is almost unbelievable. I'm trying to understand how it happened."

"I was barely nineteen when I married and we went straight to Mariposa after the wedding," she returned in her crispest tone. "Apart from David, I knew no one for thousands of miles and I didn't speak Spanish."

David had had some small knowledge of the language—enough, she discovered later, to turn down all invitations from the warmly hospitable Mariposans in the district.

She went on doggedly, "I couldn't walk anywhere—the distances are too great."

"Your parents? The estancia has a computer. Were you in contact with them?"

"They didn't have a computer and I couldn't ring—the telephone system was chancy at the best."

And what could her parents have done? Even if she'd appealed to them they didn't have the money to pay for her to go home.

Her upwards glance clashed with Rafe's burnished, metallic survey. In that cool, judicial voice he stated, "And I don't suppose you had any money."

Words froze on her tongue and she had to swallow to ease her parched throat. "No," she admitted. "I was far too young—too unsophisticated—to deal with it. My parents adored each other—and David said he loved me and wanted to keep me safe. I knew something was wrong, but I had no weapons to fight him."

"What were your parents thinking of to let you get married so young?"

She shrugged. "They married young and it worked for them. But I was the one who insisted on it. I wanted a home, somewhere to call my own, where I could make a place for myself. Each year my parents chose a place to stay over the winter, so I had time to make friends and enjoy going to school instead of doing correspondence lessons. Then in the spring we'd leave. My friends and I would promise to keep in touch, but eventually the letters would stop and I'd have to start all over again. So I married the first man who offered me a settled life."

"Did you love him?"

Her smile was wry. "I was sure I did. My parents really liked David and they thought Mariposa was a wonderful idea, that at last I was showing some adventurous spirit. And it seemed so romantic." She allowed herself a small, cynical smile. "For the right man and the right woman, it could be. For me the estancia was literally a prison. I was so lonely. When I made him angry David would disappear for days and days, and I'd be left in silence and isolation. I didn't know how to deal with it."

A cool breath from the sea made her shiver. Rafe said abruptly, "We'll go inside."

"No, I'd rather stay here." Where she could breathe. After a few seconds' pause, she resumed quietly, "Then I got pregnant. David didn't want the baby. I lost it in the first trimester, and he said it was a relief—he was happy with the way things were. He didn't ever want children."

For a moment she thought Rafe was going to speak, but when she glanced at him his face was carved in stone.

Marisa stiffened her spine, squared her shoulders. Her voice was sombre and harsh with memories. "That was when I realised that I'd never have anyone to love—no child to love me. It was the last straw. I slid into depression and when he made it impossible for me to go home after my mother became ill I was too numb to even fight any longer. I just wanted to die."

Silence, heavy with unspoken thoughts, stretched between them. She looked down at her hands, so tightly clasped together that the knuckles were white, and forced herself to drop them into her lap. "But then you came and I saw an opportunity."

His arrival had cut through the stifling oblivion of her days, offering a tantalising, life-saving chance of freedom. "Besides, I thought I might be pregnant again, so I knew I had to take any chance I could to get away."

"You said David wasn't violent, so why do you believe he'd have harmed his own child?"

"He wouldn't have hurt him physically," she said quickly, then paused. She met his gaze without flinching. "At least, I don't think so. But there are different ways to hurt. Children don't flourish in a dictatorship."

"So you told him we'd slept together and the child was mine."

His voice was neutral, but the icy depths of his eyes told her he was holding himself on a tight rein.

"I couldn't think of anything else to do," she admitted bleakly. "About a month after I'd got back to New Zealand he rang and demanded I go back to him. By then I knew for certain I was pregnant. I was—desperate. My parents needed me and the thought of returning to Mariposa filled me with a kind of terror. I did the only thing I could think of to make sure David would never want to claim my baby. I used you and it worked."

She hesitated, then confessed on a spurt of raw honesty, "I wish I could say I regret it, but I don't. I'd do it again in a blink to keep Keir safe."

Rafe's face remained emotionless—an arrogant study carved in granite.

Nerves jumping, she finished, "Rafe, I am so sorry I involved you. But it shouldn't be a problem—no one else knows…"

Her voice trailed away as she recalled his statement that in Mariposa people assumed she had slept with him.

He said without inflection, "No one else is sure, but it seems to be accepted that he left Mariposa because you and I had an affair."

"He's left Mariposa?" Her voice shook and she jumped to her feet, staring at him in shock. "When?"

"About six months after you did." He stood too, a formidable silhouette in the dimness of the terrace. Relentlessly he demanded, "Why are you so afraid? If he doesn't want children, then surely Keir is safe enough even if Brown does find out the boy is his."

Fear hollowing her stomach, Marisa gathered her thoughts, trying to adjust to the news. A gull cried in the distance, harshly distinctive, and she shivered.

"I think he saw me as some kind of chattel," she said after several silent moments. "Love for him meant—*means*—ownership, not respect. He grew up in a foster home where he had to fight to keep anything. I'm afraid that if he ever finds out that Keir is his he'll want to own him too."

Rafe's survey was keen and hard to bear, but his thoughtful answer made her hope he was beginning to understand. "That seems rather melodramatic."

She shrugged. "I don't pretend to understand him. What I'm certain of is that men like David don't make good husbands or fathers. You know Keir—he's a bright, happy, confident child. You must remember what I was like after just two years spent with David. Although, to be fair," she added with unsparing candour, "that wasn't entirely his fault."

Rafe's brows lifted again. "No?"

"No. When I got back to New Zealand my mother insisted I see her doctor. He sent me off for tests and they finally decided that a mixture of depression and chaotic hormones after the miscarriage had dragged me down. Medication and a good therapist fixed me."

"With some effort from you," he said quietly.

She nodded. "Lots of effort," she agreed.

"Tell me one thing."

The almost casual tone was so much at variance with his hard scrutiny that she tensed. "What?"

"How did Marisa turn into Mary—the name change, I mean, not the emotional disintegration?"

She flushed, but said coolly enough, "David thought Marisa was a silly, pretentious name, so he chose another one." Like renaming a pet…

Rafe nodded, as though the answer had confirmed something for him. He didn't comment, however, but moved on. "Before we finish this, I'd like to know why you came to Tewaka."

It wasn't exactly an order, but she owed him an answer to that too. At least this one was easy, she thought mordantly.

"I've always loved Northland. Having parents who made a living by catering to people's tastes gave me a feeling for what sells and what doesn't, and the shop seemed like a missed opportunity."

"In what way?"

"Poor buying," she explained. "I researched Tewaka and found it has a six-month season of cruise-ship visits as well as a year-long tourist trade, and the district is prosperous. Small shops like mine can't compete with the big chain retailers, so they need to cater for a different market. Which was what my parents did with their handmade stuff." She gave him a taut, glittering smile. "One thing I did *not* learn from my research was that you lived here."

One black brow shot up. "Would that have killed the deal?"

"Yes. I felt—still feel—guilty about using you. When my father died last year I decided to leave the south. It holds bad memories. David is from there, my parents died there and I wanted to find a place where no one would know me. Where I could make a new beginning."

"I can understand that," he said unexpectedly.

Disconcerted, Marisa looked at him and then hastily away again. While they'd been talking dusk had given way to night. Soon the moon would rise, but for now the velvet sky was spangled with stars. Her dark-attuned eyes clearly made out the arrogant bone structure of Rafe's face, the width of his shoulders against the fall of white blooms from a creeper along the wall. Something stirred deep inside her, a slow, sensuous melting, as though a resistance she'd hadn't known existed was being smoothed away.

Steadying her voice, she went on, "I wanted to settle before Keir started school. And once I started the process, everything just fell into place—it was so simple I got the feeling it was meant to be, you know?"

Only to fall spectacularly apart as soon as she'd learned he lived here.

With a twist to his mouth he said, "I'm always suspicious of deals that seem to come together perfectly. Usually it's because someone's manipulating things to their own advantage."

"Not in this case." She gave him a rueful smile. "I'd been here several weeks before I found out you lived here and my first instinct was to get the hell out of town. But Keir loves the school here and the shop is going so well." And she'd been told Rafe was rarely at home. Quickly she went on, "Anyway, I was pretty sure I could carry off my new identity. What made you recognise me? I hope there's very little resemblance between poor Mary Brown and me."

"It seems that the poor Mary Brown you refer to so disparagingly could well have saved my life. For which I'm grateful."

The tone in which he drawled the final sentence jolted her senses to overstretched alertness. Was this the only reason he'd been so helpful towards her?

A pang of disappointment shocked her with its intensity.

If he'd gone to Mariposa to find out what had happened after the crash, something she'd said or done must have aroused his suspicion.

Banishing that entirely inappropriate chagrin, she said on a note of humour, "I'll make a bargain with you. I'll stop thanking you if you stop thanking me."

"Done!" He held out his hand, and she put hers in it, ready for the sizzle of response that ran through her whenever he touched her.

It happened, but this time she didn't jerk away.

As their hands parted he said, "Although offering you a refuge is hardly recompense for saving my life. It never occurred to you to leave me in the wreckage of the plane?"

Amazed, she stared at him. "No. It wasn't an option. You sort of came to while I was checking the pilot and you muttered something about fire, and then I smelt petrol—"

"Avgas," he corrected with a half-smile.

"Whatever. It smelt like an explosion to me. You were set on getting out and it seemed a really good idea. Do you remember any of that?"

"No," he said briefly. "Finding the hut in the storm must have been difficult."

She recalled it only too vividly. "It wasn't easy. I was afraid the effort would be bad for you, but although you were obviously in pain you were so determined to get to the hut I realised you'd set off by yourself if I didn't come with you."

"Apart from the blow to my head I had no injuries," he said shortly.

"I thought the hut would be a better bet than staying in a plane that might explode." She returned to her question. "You barely saw me in Mariposa and most of the time you did you were more or less unconscious. How did you recognise me?"

"Your eyes," he said succinctly. He reached out and traced an eyebrow, his lean forefinger leaving a trail of fire on her skin. His voice deepened. "Such a strong, true green is unusual enough, but the way they tilt—and the way your brows follow that tilt—that's both exotic and unforgettable."

His touch transformed that insidious melting sensation into swift heat that ricocheted from nerve-end to nerve-end right throughout her body, sending signals to every cell.

"I have my grandmother's eyes," she said inanely.

The way he looked at her built that inner, shameless heat into a fire. Desperate to quench it, she blurted, "How did you find out about the lie I told David?"

"You told me."

Bewildered, Marisa stared at him. "But you knew before then, surely?"

His mouth curved in a sardonic smile. "I knew what he—and most of Mariposa, apparently—believes. I was intrigued by your attitude—a mixture of forthrightness and extreme caution and reserve. And I couldn't work out why the hell you'd pretend to be someone else, if that's what you were doing, unless you were afraid or had something to hide."

"So you had me investigated." She tried to sound angry, but her tone was resigned.

Hooded eyes never leaving her face, he nodded. "And discovered you'd given no name for his father on Keir's birth certificate. I wondered why."

She said nothing and after a few seconds he resumed, "Keir was born two weeks short of nine months after the night you and I spent together in the hut, so he could have been the result of one night of amnesiac passion on my part."

"No," she said decisively.

"In Mariposa I found out that we'd been naked—"

Hot-cheeked, she corrected, "*You* were naked."

"The general opinion seems to be that of course we slept together. Such a life-affirming activity is quite natural—even normal—after a fatal crash."

His words were delivered in a silky voice that froze Marisa. But only for a moment. The shock of his knowing had receded and she asked angrily, "What I'd like to know is how everyone—*everyone* meaning everyone in your circle, I assume—knew that."

"The people who rescued us talked, of course," he said caustically. "That's why your ex-husband believed you."

Anger dying, she absorbed that, then said quietly, "Keir is David's son."

"I believe you." He reached out and took her hand again. Frowning, he closed his fingers around hers. "Why didn't you tell me you were cold?"

And to her astonishment he pulled her into his arms and held her against the heat of his powerful body. "It's all right," he said evenly, his voice reverberating against her ear. "I'm sorry to take you through this inquisition, but I needed to know what was going on."

She couldn't think, couldn't tease out a sensible answer. A fierce desire clamoured through her, weakening her so that her words were husky and hesitant when she finally blurted, "I'm not cold—just…shocked, I suppose."

"Too much has happened to you lately."

His arms contracted and she looked up, eyes widening as she met the focused gleam in his. She shivered again.

He bent his head and said against lips that ached for some unknown pressure, "After the crash you risked your life to warm me. I wonder if I can warm you up this time."

The kiss rekindled the fires, setting her alight with the passion she'd been fighting ever since she'd seen him again. Sighing, she surrendered to a sharp excitement, a reckless need that came roaring up out of nowhere, summoned by Rafe's touch, his arms, his lips…

Summoned by Rafe.

Desire burnt through her, his mouth on hers causing a conflagration, a violent force that swept away everything but hunger and the ruthless, wildfire longing. Stunned by its intensity, a flash of insight made Marisa face the truth—this heady clamour was what had broken through her inertia in Mariposa. Involuntarily her body had reacted to Rafe's compelling magnetism, stimulating her into the action that had finally freed her.

She wanted more of it… She opened her mouth beneath his insistent demand and he took immediate advantage of the silent plea. The deep kiss that followed caused a peak of sensation, robbing her of all thought, all emotion, except a voluptuous craving unlike anything she'd ever experienced.

She almost cried out when he lifted his head.

"I'm sorry," he said harshly, and let her go, stepping back several paces as though he needed to put space between them.

"Sorry? *Sorry?*" She said unsteadily, "Why—why did you stop?"

CHAPTER NINE

RAFE bit back an oath. *Way to go, you fool*, he thought grimly, looking down at her, the soft lips trembling, her eyes wide and dazed.

The last thing you should be doing is kissing her like some lust-crazed idiot after she's just relived as nasty a case of emotional abuse as you've ever heard.

His voice harsh, he said, "Now is not the time. You've been through hell—"

Marisa crossed the space between them, reached up and put her hand across his mouth. "You're the first man who's touched me since I left Mariposa." She gave a twisted smile. "I used you, lied about you. I'm not going to lie again. I want you too."

Other women had come on to Rafe, some with disconcerting directness, most with considerably more subtlety, but none had made him feel like this. Marisa's touch, her words, sent desire pouring through him so that he had to grit his teeth to stop himself from losing control.

"Are you sure?" he demanded, his voice low and feral.

She dropped her hand. "Sure that I want you? Completely." Her voice shook and heat swept along her perfect cheekbones, but her gaze was honest.

"Why?" And why the hell was he probing? In his previous affairs all he'd expected was mutual desire. Now he wanted more—without knowing what that *more* would be.

The question shocked Marisa like a bucket of water in the face, jolting her out of her sensuous haze.

Panicked, she thought, *However much I want to, I can't do this.* Whatever Rafe was offering, it wouldn't be permanence… She was not only gambling with her life, she was gambling with Keir's.

Yet a flicker of subversive regret made her wonder if she was going to remain celibate until her son grew up.

Ashamed, colour flaring up through her skin, she said awkwardly, "I wish you hadn't asked that—but I'm glad you did. I don't have just myself to think about. Keir is becoming fond of you and it's going to hurt him when we leave." Desperation tinged her voice. "I have to find somewhere else to live!"

Rafe's intent, probing gaze, colder than an Antarctic sky in winter, seemed to pierce the façade she'd manufactured with such effort and patience. Shaking with the need to surrender, she watched him re-impose control and wished forlornly that it could be as easy for her.

"In that case," he said coolly, "I'll stay away as much as I can while you're here."

She firmed her mouth, knowing it was the best thing he could do. "Yes," she said colourlessly. "Thank you."

She looked up and met his level, iron-grey gaze. Deep inside her something contracted, almost banishing her tiredness in a surge of heat.

"Goodnight," she said and shot through the door, closing it behind her and leaning back against it, her heart pounding so noisily in her chest she could hear nothing else.

Of course Keir's welfare was the most important factor in her life. Yet for a moment she wondered what it would be like to be able to dream of something else, something for herself…

Sleep refused to come. Restlessly she tossed beneath the sheet, turning questions over in her mind.

What did she know about Rafe? Not enough to trust him. Oh, he was not only respected in Tewaka, he was liked—but no man could reach the heights he'd achieved without a strong streak of ruthlessness.

Why was she attracted to dominant men? She'd vowed never to allow that to happen to her again.

Yet she wanted Rafe. And he knew it. The minutes spent responding to his kisses with such passionate abandon had given her away completely.

Wildly successful, magnetic, brilliant, worldly—she could probably spend the rest of what promised to be a long and sleepless night thinking up words to describe him, but they all meant the same thing.

The good fairies around his cradle had showered him with more gifts than necessary. He could have any woman in the world.

Which was probably why he'd pulled back when she'd turned to jelly in his arms.

It was so…so *unlikely* that he'd want someone like her, not only scarred emotionally, but so very ordinary.

Unless he still wondered if Keir might be his son? Perhaps that was why he'd invited them to stay at Manuwai?

That thought made her feel sick, but it had to be faced.

She went over the conversation, testing everything Rafe had said. It was possible he did wonder…

Where was David now? Hot and sticky, she turned her pillow over and kicked off the sheet. Outside the little owl the Maori had named *ruru* was calling from a nearby tree. *Morepork, morepork*—a lonely, familiar sound, one she'd heard all over New Zealand, yet in the pleasant bedroom Marisa shivered.

Tomorrow she'd have plenty to face; right now she needed sleep.

Eventually it came.

Keir woke her, saying urgently, "Mum, it's late. You better get up now. The sun has got his smiley face on."

She bolted upright, checked the clock and said something under her breath, then huffed out a sigh and relaxed. "Today's Sunday, you horrible boy," she said affectionately. "It's a holiday. No shop and no school."

He grinned. "We can go down to the beach and swim all day," he suggested eagerly. "After we have pancakes for breakfast with lemon juice and brown sugar?"

Laughing, she threw back the sheet and swung out of bed, ruffling his hair as she went past him. "First I have to shower and get dressed."

At least, she thought a few minutes later, she didn't have to worry too much about what she would wear to face Rafe again. Jeans and a well-worn T-shirt that echoed the colour of her eyes would have to do.

Not too long afterwards she and Keir walked into the kitchen. Rafe looked around from the counter, where he was setting up the coffee machine.

"Good morning," he said, that perceptive gaze going from Marisa's guarded face to Keir's delighted one.

Keir ran across the room, his pleasure so patent it wrung Marisa's heart.

"I didn't know you were here," he said exuberantly. "Did you come home on the helicopter last night? Did you fly it?"

"No and no," Rafe said calmly. "The chopper's having a check-up so I came home by car after you were asleep. How have you been? Has your car arrived back with a new starter motor?"

"Yes, but I liked your grandma's car better, only Mum says we have to drive our own one again."

As she busied herself making pancake batter, Marisa listened to the two of them talking and thought miserably that if only she and Rafe had made love on that wreck of a bed in the hut…

A voluptuous need coiled through her, seductive as the original serpent. *Don't go there*, she thought feverishly.

But if Keir were Rafe's son, his future would be assured.

If only she didn't feel this scary, primal attraction… Every time she saw Rafe her brain went mushy, tempting her in so many dangerous ways.

She switched on the gas, coated a pan with butter and waited for it to sizzle before ladling in the batter.

"Pancakes?" Rafe said thoughtfully. "They're one of my favourite breakfasts."

Ever helpful, Keir said, "Then Mummy can make some for you."

Marisa looked up, saw a glint in Rafe's eyes and smiled, a dangerous expectation scintillating through her like diamond dust in her blood. "I made enough batter for us all," she told him.

Rafe cocked a sardonic brow, but remained silent.

The faint shadows beneath Marisa's eyes were more than enough evidence of a wakeful night.

His gut tightened as he thought of another way she could have spent those hours of darkness—a much more satisfactory way for both of them. The kisses he'd exchanged with her had left him hungry and frustrated in the most basic way, killing sleep until late.

He was a sophisticated man—not promiscuous, and normal in his appetites. He liked rare steak, a good wine, the refreshment of a cool shower after exertion, the softness and passion of women. He expected to marry—some time. His parents' disastrous marriage had convinced him that a steady, safe, completely reliable affection was the best basis for a lifelong relationship.

What he'd never anticipated was this smouldering hunger that wouldn't leave him alone.

Had the situation been normal, Marisa would have spent last night in his bed, in his arms. His body tightened, but he ignored it. Her revelation about her marriage complicated everything. Rafe killed a primitive urge to make David Brown pay for the emotional pain he'd inflicted.

Any further advance in their mutual attraction would have to be on Marisa's terms, not his. And she'd made it very clear that for her, young Keir's welfare came before everything else.

They ate out on the terrace, the sun beaming down on them like a benediction, and the motionless branches of the pohutukawa trees spangled with blue-green glimpses of the sea behind.

* * *

After breakfast Rafe headed off to his study. Mariposa's time zone was fifteen hours behind New Zealand's—if his luck was in, he'd get an instant answer.

Sure enough, the manager emailed back within ten minutes. Rafe's frown grew darker as he read the answer. *You may remember he lit a fire in the machinery shed. When questioned, he said it was to make a point, but that he didn't intend to harm anyone. The previous agent believed this.*

Rafe could almost feel the agent's curiosity smoking off the screen, but contented himself with a terse note of thanks. An odd sensation of foreboding gripping him, he left the computer and walked across to the huge kauri desk his father had worked at, like his forefathers before him. Making up his mind, he lifted the telephone and punched in a number.

He listened to what his private investigator had to say with a gathering grimness.

After a short conversation he put down the phone and strode across to the window to stare unseeingly out.

His strong sense that something was wrong had stood him in good stead before. He'd learned to pay careful attention to it.

He found Marisa with Keir in the garden. "We need to talk," he told her and switched his gaze to Keir, absorbed in examining a large, jazzily striped Monarch-butterfly caterpillar on the swan plant. "I've asked Ngaire Sinclair to come across with young Manu around ten; she's happy to keep the boys down on the beach until midday."

Marisa opened her mouth to object, then closed it again. If they needed to talk, it would have to be without any chance of Keir overhearing. But her stomach clamped at the thought of what lay ahead. She'd desperately wanted a peaceful day to recharge her batteries.

"All right," she agreed.

From the terrace off the small parlour Marisa watched the boys frolic around Ngaire like two puppies across the lawn and disappear down the cliff path to the children's beach. Turning, she tried to relax taut muscles. Colour stung her skin when she realised Rafe was watching her, his grey eyes coolly speculative.

Heart jumping, she said, "Something's happened. What is it?"

"Your ex-husband is somewhere in New Zealand."

She flinched as though struck by a blow. Rafe had to rein in a fierce, intemperate anger. The man might not have hit her, but she was actively afraid of him.

"How—?" She stopped, cleared her throat and firmed her lush mouth into a straight line. "How do you know?" she demanded.

He frowned, "Come inside. You're shivering."

Silently she accompanied him into the house. Once inside one look at her convinced him this was hugely unpleasant news. Her eyes were blank in her white face, but as he watched she gave herself a little shake and some colour came back into her skin.

Tight-lipped, he said, "I thought you knew that. You divorced him a couple of years after he left Mariposa."

"That was done through lawyers," she shot back. "He had a lawyer in Invercargill. I certainly didn't know he was here in New Zealand."

"He went to Australia first," Rafe said, watching her closely.

Her relief was patent, but it didn't last long. She

looked up at him. "When did he come back to New Zealand?"

"When you moved north to Tewaka."

The little colour in her skin leached away and she sent an involuntary glance towards the beach as though she thought her ex-husband might be there, threatening their son.

Once more Rafe watched her get a grip on her fears. "How do you know all this?" she asked in a quiet voice very much at variance with that first moment of panic.

"Sit down," he ordered.

She gave him a speaking glance, but sat down in the chair. "I'll be back in a moment," he said and strode through to the other room.

Marisa was sitting very erect when he came back, but there was an emptiness in the green eyes he recognised, and her soft mouth was held in firm restraint. No woman should ever look like that. He reined in his anger and handed her the glass.

She took it automatically, and sipped, then choked. "Ugh!" she spluttered. "What *is* this?"

"Brandy. Drink at least some of it. You've had a shock and it will help."

"Not to keep a clear head, it won't," she said, and put it down. She fixed him with a determined stare. "You didn't answer my question. How do you know all this?"

"I employ an extremely experienced firm of private investigators to check up on anything I need to know," he said, half-amused by her attempt to wrest control of the situation from him.

Half-amused, impressed—and secretly frustrated as hell.

Because his body still thrummed with a ruthless

need. But that wildfire hunger was backed by a strong urge to protect her and the boy.

She frowned, her lips easing into a faint, humourless smile. "Yes, of course you do. Are they so good you know where David is now?"

"Not that good," he acknowledged drily. "In Australia he was working on a cattle station in the Outback. He flew to New Zealand about a month ago, landing in Christchurch. Since then, nothing."

Which possibly meant he was travelling under an assumed name.

She drew in a sharp breath. "I could try his lawyer."

"Even if they're still in touch, his solicitor isn't likely to tell you unless you can give a damned good reason. Like the fact that Brown is Keir's father…" Deliberately he let the words trail off.

"That's never going to happen," she asserted fiercely.

"In that case, stay away from his solicitor."

Narrow black brows met for a moment and then she agreed, "You're right, I'd be stupid to make any contact."

Her hands clenched together in her lap. She raised her dark green gaze to meet his and said bleakly, "It's all right. I'll work something out."

His voice raw, he said, "Hell! You're not just afraid of him, you're terrified."

Marisa looked away, but he caught her chin in a firm grip and turned her face towards him. The heat faded from her skin. Unable to answer, she nervously swallowed and he let her go.

"Yes," he said, as if somehow she'd confirmed it. "Why? He has no power over you now."

Buffeted by his formidable determination, she couldn't assemble any coherent answer from the disconnected fragments of thought that tumbled and jostled through her mind. When she did find her voice it sounded weak and ineffectual. "If he ever finds out that Keir is his, he'd fight me for him." She glanced up at him, eyes shadowy and troubled. "Rafe, this is not your battle, even though I involved you in it."

"I want to know why you're so afraid of this man," he stated, not giving an inch. "Have you told me everything? You're a strong woman—yet you're terrified of him. Even if he does discover that Keir is his son and gain access, you'd be able to monitor the situation."

Surrendering, she dragged in a breath. "I suppose I'm as much afraid of myself as I am of him," she said, her voice rough. "I married him as a normal nineteen-year-old and within two years I was a wreck. Loneliness was a big part of it. But there were other things—little things…"

Her voice died away.

"Go on," Rafe said steadily.

She summoned her courage. "One of the men brought me a parrot—a little gold-and-blue bird that lives in the trees by the streams and can be taught to talk. It had fallen out of the nest somehow and I nursed it back to health, but almost as soon as it started to repeat the words I was teaching it, it died. He wouldn't let me see the body. He just told me about it and then he buried it. I didn't think anything of it. Then there was a kitten. It was fine one day, playing at my feet, but it died overnight too."

Although she paused, Rafe remained silent, the only sign of any reaction the thinning of his mouth. So she went on, "He promised me a puppy to replace it, but it never arrived…"

She glanced up, saw him frown and went on starkly,

"And painting—he referred to it as a hobby, but as the months went by it became my lifeline. When I ran out of paints he said he'd ordered more, but none ever came. I wish I could explain just how empty I felt with nothing to do except housework, nobody to talk to except him. There were no books and he didn't see any reason for a garden…" Her voice tailed away.

Rafe said, "Go on."

"I wanted to learn Spanish; he thought—or said he thought—it would be a good idea. He was learning quite a bit from the men, but he was always too tired to teach me and he didn't want me talking to the men. He used to read my parents' letters, so I couldn't say anything to them." She made a swift gesture of despair. "It sounds petty and foolish—"

"It sounds like a reign of terror," Rafe said grimly. "What about his parents? Were you in contact with them?"

"Oh, no. David never knew his birth parents—he was given up for adoption as a baby. But something happened when he was seven—I don't know what—and he spent the rest of his childhood in foster homes. Some were good, but he never stayed long enough in one to really find a home."

"Why?"

She shrugged. "I don't know. He didn't like talking about it. He told me he had to be tough; when he was hurt he didn't rest until he'd paid people back, punishing them, because that way they left him alone. And if—if he still feels that way, what better way to punish me than try to take Keir away?"

Recounting this took all of her courage, but she owed Rafe. She finished, "Keir is starting to look more and more like him. If he forced me to allow Keir to be DNA tested he'd discover the truth." She lifted her gaze at Rafe, searching his hard, arrogant face for some sign of understanding. "You called it a reign of terror. That's what I'm afraid of—the damage he might be able to do to Keir's peace of mind, his lovely, sunny personality..." She blinked back tears and said fiercely, "I'll do anything I can to make sure it doesn't happen."

"I see now why you don't want him in Keir's life, but if he did apply, he'd almost certainly get access." Rafe spoke objectively, clearly weighing the information. "Your lies would put you in an unfavourable position."

Bleakly she admitted, "I know. Do you think I don't worry about what I've done? I do. That lie has weighed on my shoulders ever since I told it." She caught her breath and held her head high, meeting his eyes with a defiance based on fear. "But I'd do it again. Is it too much to want Keir to have a serene childhood, one where he can grow up and be happy and not be burdened with adult problems? You know him—does he seem to be missing anything?"

"Not obviously, no." Rafe paced across to the window, big and lithe and predatory. Once there he swung around and surveyed her, his expression closed. "But that could change. Children are said to need a stable male figure in their lives. If it did come to a custody dispute, you'd be in a much stronger position if there was a man in your life, someone Keir liked and respected." He paused, before saying calmly, "The simplest way to ensure that would be for us to get engaged."

Marisa stared at him, his words dancing crazily through her head. It took every ounce of self-control to say, "No, no, that's not necessary."

"It makes sense," he said coolly, his mouth twisting

as he took in her patent shock. "If it does nothing else, it will reinforce the idea that the boy is mine."

"Yes, but there's absolutely no reason for you to be involved—"

"You involved me when you came up with that lie," he told her uncompromisingly.

Colour burned her skin, then faded. She couldn't refute that.

Before she could come up with a reply, he said, "You can't admit to the lie without possibly jeopardising Keir's well-being, so you might as well make use of it again."

Marisa shook her head, swamped by bone-deep exhaustion.

Rafe touched her shoulder, then dropped his hand. "You're exhausted and no wonder. Drink some more brandy." His tone was remote and decisive, as though working out some strategy.

Nerves jumping in a complex mixture of tension and dismay—and something deeper, more basic, that she wasn't prepared to explore—she tried to match his judicial tone. "I don't need brandy, thanks. And I can't believe that being engaged to you would sway a family court."

"You'd be surprised," he said cynically, adding in a gentler voice, "Marisa, try not to worry. We don't know that Brown is interested in establishing contact with Keir. We'll discuss this further when you've had time to think things over."

Not if she could prevent it. All she wanted to do was crawl into some hole, pull the door shut behind her and stay there until this whole thing went away.

If it ever did…

But Rafe's use of *we* comforted her.

The sound of children's voices dragged her gaze towards the garden. Surely it wasn't lunchtime—no, Ngaire was piggybacking young Manu.

Galvanised, she said, "Something's happened to Manu, I think."

"Probably a cut from a shell. I'll get the first-aid kit."

Before he left she said in a muted voice, "Rafe, when you told me David was back in New Zealand I panicked. All this time I'd presumed he was still in Mariposa, you see, which is why I didn't—*couldn't*—tell you who I was."

"I understand that your son's welfare is the most important thing in your life."

He sounded completely in command, as though it was quite ordinary to propose a fake engagement with a woman he barely knew to safeguard a child who wasn't his own.

CHAPTER TEN

THE children were so disappointed by the early cessation of their stay on the beach that Ngaire said, "Look, why don't you let Keir come home with us? Quite frankly, it would be a good thing. Manu's going to have to keep off that heel for the rest of the day, so he and Keir can watch a DVD together. I'll drop Keir off around four?"

At Keir's exuberant little jump, Marisa laughed. "You have your answer. Thanks very much, he'd love to come."

Which left her alone in the house with Rafe. However, he retired to his office, emerging for lunch with an abstracted air and returning immediately afterwards. She told herself she was relieved. Feeling awkward was irritating and she refused to accept that she had any reason for it.

The problem was it wouldn't go away.

When he walked out and found her bringing in a load of washing from the line, he asked, "Surely Nadine can do that?"

"These are our sheets," she said firmly. "And our clothes." She folded one of Keir's small shirts and put it over the top of a lacy bra.

A smile curved Rafe's mouth, but he said, "Have you made up your mind yet? Are we engaged or not?"

At the sardonic note in his voice her stomach went into free fall. "Oh, don't be silly," she blurted, then could have kicked herself for coming up with such an unsophisticated retort. "You know it's not at all necessary."

"I'm beginning to feel it's very necessary," he said curtly, eyes never leaving her face.

Eyes widening, she stared at him, a torrent of thoughts cascading through her mind. "You've heard where he is," she breathed.

He shook his black head. "No." Then paused, as though weighing his words.

His tone was level, perfectly steady, yet when she looked at him an emotion close to fear chilled her.

"But I've just been talking to the chief of the local fire brigade."

"You don't need to tell me—you went to school with him," she said brightly, sensing he was about to tell her something she didn't want to hear.

His smile was brief and unamused. "As it happens, yes, I did. He said the first fire—the cottage—was probably caused by a cigarette thrown from a car. The long grass at the fence line caught and it got to the house. The garage might be arson."

She blinked and felt her muscles sag. When he took a step towards her she stiffened, straightening her spine and warding him off with a rapid, involuntary gesture. He stopped a pace away.

"Kids?" she hazarded tautly. "Bored teenagers?"

"Possibly." He paused, then said, "Your ex-husband was sacked from the estancia because he burned down the machinery shed shortly after you told him I was

Keir's father. He didn't intend to harm anyone, but one of the farmhands had a narrow escape."

Marisa could feel the colour drain from her skin, leaving her cold and shaken. "Who?" she breathed, her mind ranging over the farmhands.

He looked surprised. "I don't know—whoever it was got out just in time. As far as I know he wasn't hurt."

Before she could say anything he continued, "One of the Tanner boys looked out the night the garage burned down and saw a vehicle parked by it. He thought it was another volunteer checking the cottage. However, the brigade had left, convinced there was no further chance of the place catching fire."

"And you think…" Marisa searched for words, but could only shake her head.

His gaze still on her face, Rafe went on, "You told me Brown rang you about a month after you'd come back to New Zealand to be with your parents."

"Yes."

"And that was when you told him you'd slept with me and that the baby you were having was mine?"

His coolly judicial voice steadied her.

"Yes," she repeated numbly.

"He lit the fire five weeks after you'd left him."

Marisa's teeth clamped down on her bottom lip. "Oh, heavens," she whispered. "Rafe, I'm so sorry."

He shrugged. "It's not your fault. I assume he tried to pay me back in the only way he could—by destroying something of mine. If he set the garage alight, he'd be punishing you by destroying something of yours."

"But we don't know… I can't believe…" Her incredulous voice trailed away, because it made a hideous sort of sense.

"I think you do," Rafe said, mercilessly refusing to

offer any sort of comfort. "Why else would you be so afraid he might find out Keir is his child? You sensed he was capable of violence."

"I didn't—" She stopped, met his dispassionate gaze and expelled a long, sobbing breath, facing the truth at last. "Yes. Yes, of course I did. But I can't believe he'd try to *kill* anyone."

"Whoever lit these fires didn't intend to kill," he said crisply. "The danger comes when a fire gets out of control. Or when people aren't where arsonists expect them to be—as happened in Mariposa."

A pause made it obvious he expected a reply, but Marisa remained silent, grappling with the implications of this. From somewhere close by a seagull called, its screech a threat and a warning. She shivered, and hugged herself, rubbing her hands over her suddenly cold arms.

After a few seconds Rafe continued, "Of course this is all supposition. We don't have a single fact to go on beyond that he admitted to lighting a fire in the machine shed in Mariposa. But your instincts are good. You recognised something about him that convinced you he'd never be a good father."

She nodded. "What…what I'm trying to work out is how I can deal with this."

"*We* are going to become engaged," he said deliberately, emphasising the first word. "Then, if it's necessary, I can protect you and Keir."

"That's outrageously noble of you," she fired back, so tempted to surrender it was difficult to get the words out. "But nobody gets engaged for such quixotic reasons."

Rafe's smile curled her toes. "I can be as foolish as

the next man," he drawled and took the shirt she'd just unpegged and tossed it into the clothes basket.

He drew her towards him, but although she longed for his mouth on hers, his arms didn't tighten around her and he said above her head, "If it is arson, and if it is your ex, an engagement to me is likely to be as good a protection for young Keir and you as anything else."

Better, she thought, trying to resist the powerful, honey-and-flame rush of desire she'd been longing for through the night.

And not just last night.

Without realising it, she'd spent the past five years missing the primal security she'd once felt in Rafe's arms. Locked against his lean, strong body while the rain hammered down outside the hut, she'd inhaled the faint, unmistakably masculine perfume of his skin, listened to his regular breathing, been reassured by the steady beat of his heart. And in those long hours, some essential, unknown part of her had surrendered.

Yet it was more than a simple longing for a safe haven…

He'd roused a sleeping hunger in her, an appetite both erotic and emotional—something she'd refused to admit even to herself. Only when she'd seen him again had that forbidden yearning prompted her to wonder what it would be like to share the burden, give her a chance to be more than Keir's mother and protector—to be Rafe's lover.

Now, in this perilous moment, she was given a glimpse of paradise. Rafe's embrace extinguished sanity in a surge of sensual craving, and she barely had time to think, *I mustn't let this happen*, before he tilted her head and examined her face. Heat kindled in his iron-grey eyes and that dangerous, voluptuous yearning overwhelmed her as he took her mouth.

Last night their kisses had been measured, almost experimental. Rafe had explored her lips with assurance and sensuous, erotically charged skill, but she'd been wary, unable to resist, yet not ready to yield to headstrong temptation.

This was different. This time when he kissed her a surge of reckless delight persuaded her to open her lips, to savour his taste as though she'd hungered for it all her life.

His reaction was instantaneous, close to ruthless. With their bodies sealed together as though nothing could ever separate them again, Marisa dug her fingers into the hard muscles of his back with an abandon that felt so good, so completely right.

When at last he lifted his head, her knees buckled and she had to cling desperately.

He held her effortlessly and said on a harsh, raw note, "Marisa."

She looked up into grey eyes, stormy as the clouds that lashed Mariposa in the rainy season. They locked on to hers, probing through to her soul.

Fiercely pleased, she said, "What is it?"

"What you do to me," he muttered and lowered his head again.

She shivered with desperate delight when he kissed her throat and the silky, sensuous spot below her ear, a soft kiss that sent rills of voluptuous anticipation aching through her. Deep in the pit of her stomach a deeper, more primitive sensation tightened into hunger.

His hand slid down to cup her breast. Instantly the rills turned to torrents that drowned her in acute, almost painful anticipation, contracted every pleading muscle with the need to find—to find a place where she could give in to the desire that consumed her with reckless, compelling power.

It would be so easy to stop thinking, to give in to the heady clamour of her body—to make love with Rafe…

Keir, she thought desperately.

Shocked, shamed by her easy surrender, she tried to wrench herself away. Rafe's arms tightened instinctively, but after only a second he let her go. He didn't move; when she took an uncertain, wavering step back his hand shot out to steady her.

"What is it?" he demanded forcefully.

"No," she gabbled, searching the harsh, beautiful contours of his face. "No, we can't do this. It's…it's…" She searched for the correct word, finally blurting, "It's dangerous."

"Not in my book."

His voice was hard and arrogant. It should have frozen her desire, but when she saw her own need echoed in the dark intensity of his gaze she shivered again, fighting herself and the impetuous demands of her body.

"And what is dangerous?" he demanded. "Making love? Or becoming engaged?"

"Both," she flung at him, closing her eyes against his face in case it torpedoed her resolution. "But especially getting engaged. Too many things could go wrong."

"Name one."

She seized on the most painful. "Keir. He's already learning to love you. When we leave I know now he'll be upset, but he knows—I've told him several times—that we're just on holiday here, not going to stay. If he thinks there's a chance we might live here with you all the time, he'll be heartbroken. I don't want him to end up like a child from a broken home."

"He's already from a broken home," he said curtly.

Marisa closed her eyes against this blunt, cruel statement and pulled air into her lungs by sheer force of will. "Until I saw him with you I didn't realise how much he's been missing a father. To find one in you, then to be torn away from you—I couldn't put him through that again."

"Again?" he asked sharply.

She nodded. "He grieved for my mother after her death, but he was heartbroken when Dad went—he'd been Dad's little mate."

He stepped away, leaving her suddenly cold, his expression closed against her. Quickly, before he could say anything, she blurted, "And you could meet someone and fall in love with her."

Only to have him dismiss it with quick, cold assurance. "I keep my promises."

Shocked by a lightning flash of insight, Marisa clenched her teeth on something too close to a sob. If Rafe ever loved another woman it would hurt—so much.

But it would be even worse to be engaged to him and know it was only his unsparing integrity that kept him beside her.

An acute, panicky sense of vulnerability stopped her from speaking. She'd already endured one barren relationship; she was not going to let herself be seduced into another.

Was this love...?

No. She didn't even know what love was. Whatever she'd felt for David had been false, based on her need for security. This too might be the same…

She gave him a hunted look. "Do you think I—any

woman—would be happy knowing only a promise was keeping a man beside her?"

Rafe's brows rose. "I hope that your complete lack of sense is due to raging passion," he murmured lazily, "rather than a sudden loss of brain cells. Relax—it's not going to happen. If it makes you feel any better, I'm not at all sure that I'm capable of the sort of love poets celebrate. But I can assure you I don't deliberately hurt people…and I think we have more than enough going to enjoy a very satisfactory relationship."

And he ran a forefinger from her chin down the slender column of her throat to the far-from-sexy neckline of her polo shirt.

Shivering, stunned by her body's sensuous response to that sure, sensitively judged caress, she concentrated on marshalling her thoughts into a coherent argument. "R-Rafe, this is serious. We can't play with lives like that—not Keir's, not our own. And we don't even know if getting engaged will keep David away."

His finger stilled before he lifted it to tilt her chin so that he could search her face. "I am not in the habit of playing with lives." Each word was clipped and decisive, as though her words had touched a nerve. "And if an engagement isn't likely to keep your ex-husband away, a marriage certainly would."

Marisa had to lock her knees to keep herself upright. Eyes widening, she stared at him as though he'd threatened her with a gun.

"Are you mad?" she asked faintly, managing to take one wobbly step away from him.

"I suspect I am," he said, something like humour glinting in his eyes. It disappeared quickly and in a crisp, judicial voice he said, "You have two options. You can run again and hope Brown never finds you and

Keir, or you can stay and fight this out once and for all. Hiding in New Zealand is pretty near impossible. It's too small, with too few people. Even in huge countries with large populations, it's difficult to stay hidden. If you meet him face to face, you'll feel safer with some protection. I can give you that."

"Why?" she asked starkly. "You don't really want to marry me—you don't even *know* me..."

"I know you saved my life," he said austerely. "I can imagine how hard it was for you to get me out of that plane, then support me to the hut."

He waited, but her quick brain let her down and a more primitive part adjured her to remain silent.

Crisply Rafe said, "I know you'd gladly sacrifice your life for your son. I also know loyalty like that is hard to earn and probably even harder to keep."

"Any mother would do the same," she returned with stubborn determination.

"Not all. My mother took a pay-off of ten million dollars and left without a backwards glance," he told her with savage emphasis. "I was six. I stood in the gateway and watched her drive away, knowing she'd never come back."

Mutely she nodded.

He didn't reach out to her, but his intention was as palpable as though he'd stroked her. "*I* know I want you and that the wanting grows every time I see you."

"Yes, but is that enough?" she asked impulsively, then stopped, dismayed. Her skin heated again when she met his glinting scrutiny.

Damn, she thought urgently. Oh, damn and double damn—she'd just admitted she was every bit as hungry for him as he was for her.

Not that it mattered. Rafe was a sophisticated man

and according to the media he'd enjoyed the charms of some very sophisticated women. He'd have recognised the drumming heat of carnality between them the first time they'd kissed.

"For me, yes." He shrugged. "My father fell in love with my mother and married her out of hand. It was a disaster. His second wife he chose more carefully. They built a very strong marriage and were happy."

Marisa tried to ignore the treacherous inner part of her that was ignoring all the caveats and cautions to whisper seductively *Why not...?*

Swiftly she said, "I've already made one really bad decision when I married David. Now I have to think of Keir. If things fall to pieces one day it's he who will really suffer."

Rafe said calmly, "I agree. I'm not proposing an immediate marriage. An engagement will give us time to know each other better. It will also give you time to discover whether or not you'll be happy here." Clearly he discerned her fears, because he added, "And to find out whether you've made the same mistake with me as you did before."

"I don't think so," she admitted quietly. Rafe was even more dangerous to her than David—in an entirely different way. "But what's in it for you?"

And saw with wry amusement that her directness startled him.

But only for a second. It was soon chased away by a smile that held both amusement and a certain irony. "Apart from anything else, the pleasure of knowing that no matter how much I learn about you, you're always able to surprise me."

She blinked. "I don't set out to."

"I know. That's why I enjoy it. As for the other—"

He reached for her, letting his hands rest lightly on her shoulders before pulling her slowly into his arms, giving her time to step away. “I foresee that I would enjoy being married to you very much.”

Her heart thudded to a stop, then lurched into uneven overdrive.

Eyes darkening, she froze. She couldn’t say anything, nor did she struggle when he turned her face up towards him.

“And I intend for you to enjoy it very much too,” he said with a narrowed, dangerous look that dared her to object.

And kissed her. Lost in the magic of his touch, his mouth, she spun out completely, but a tiny shred of self-control lingered, enough for her to say shakily when he lifted his head, “I d-don’t think this is a good idea.”

“Why?” he said, his mouth curving.

She dragged a breath into starving lungs, compelling her dazed, dreamy mind to concentrate. Soon, she thought hazily, soon she’d pull away, free herself from the heady exhilaration that drugged her.

“Because,” she breathed helplessly.

Rafe’s laughter was underlined by a raw note that emphasised the hardening of his body against her. He closed her eyes with quick kisses, then lowered his head and dropped more kisses on her throat.

A sensuous groan tore through Marisa, partly protest but caused by the most intense pleasure—like nothing she’d ever felt before.

It was enough to make her jerk backwards. For a heartbeat he resisted, then let her go, his expression hardening when he inspected her clouding face.

She burst into speech, trying to clear that sensuous haze from her mind. “You’re not the sort of man to marry just to help someone out. And don't give me that guff about saving your life, either—you're rich enough to give me a million dollars and not even notice it had gone. That way you could salve any feelings of gratitude without tying yourself to me and another man's child. So what's in it for you?"

"Is that what you'd rather have—a million dollars?" he asked with a mirthless, cynical smile.

"If you gave me a million dollars," she told him, parrying his hooded gaze, "I'd hand the lot to a refuge for battered women."

He flung his head back and laughed. "I suspect you would and without a second thought."

"Count on it," she told him, adding with a twisted smile, "although I can't guarantee not to give it a second thought, or even a third one. But I've learned how to live without relying on anyone else and I plan to keep on doing that. I don't want your money."

"Good, because I don't plan to give it to you. I learned the lesson my father had to learn the hard way—don't pay people off." He added on a deeper, more harsh note, "As for what's in it for me…"

He reached out for her.

Marisa's heart began to pound again. He didn't try to kiss her—he didn't even hold her tightly, yet her body ached with sweet delight at his nearness and she had to stop herself from sinking against him.

"I think you know what's in it for me," he said quietly. "And whatever it is, you feel it too."

"Lust," she said, the word stark with an obscure disappointment. What had she expected—a protestation of undying love?

It would never come from Rafe. Dared she accept his

proposition—follow this fierce longing down whatever path it led her? Dared she risk Keir's happiness?

Stupid questions. Common sense and everything she'd learned told her to refuse his proposition and walk away before she got hurt again.

Yet still she hesitated, so tempted to take a rash chance without putting her son first that she had to clench her jaw to stop the impetuous words tumbling out.

Was it too selfish to want something for herself?

Because she wanted Rafe with an intensity that made her dizzy, setting her body alight and scrambling her brain—and threatening her principles.

At least there would be honesty. Rafe had laid down his terms and she knew exactly what sort of marriage they'd have. One that was convenient for both of them. One that would provide a safe haven for Keir.

"What are you thinking?" Rafe asked.

She said, "That I need something—"

His brows rose. "What?"

Was there a hint of cynicism in his tone? Marisa thought furiously for a few seconds, then snapped her head up. "I want to make a condition. Two, actually."

CHAPTER ELEVEN

RAFE released her. Something in his expression chilled Marisa, but she went on, “I’ll understand if you refuse them. I want a promise—a *written* promise—that if you fall in love with anyone else our engagement will finish. And I want you to promise me that when we part, you’ll keep in touch with Keir. Seeing him with you has taught me that he needs a man in his life. One he can rely on. I know it’s asking a lot—”

He said nothing, and she made a gesture of negation. “Forget about it. It’s not worth the risk. We shouldn’t let this— I can’t let this…this—”

“The word *written* made me wonder if you’ve learned anything about me at all,” he said on an odd note.

His mouth crushed her answer to nothingness and the words fled from her mind. Desire was a primal need in her, a longing that brooked no restraint, a potent force that grew as their lips clung and his body hardened against her.

When he lifted his head, he said harshly, “Lust, desire, passion, hunger—who cares what name we give it?” He released her, dark eyes narrowing as he scanned her face. “It’s there and we both feel it.”

“Yes,” she said, the word a husky sigh.

It was surrender and he knew it. His gaze hardened,

heated, sending erotic shivers through her. "I agree to your conditions. So we'll go ahead with an engagement."

Bemused, her heart hammering so loudly in her chest she was sure he had to hear it, she nodded. A strange mixture of emotions coursed through her as she waited for him to pull her into his arms again with an expectancy that was as much foreboding as hope, as much fear as love.

But he made no move towards her and the heat from his kisses faded, leaving her cold from her heart out.

Rafe didn't ask for love, nor did he promise it. She honoured him for that. Perhaps this fake engagement would enable them to trust each other. They might even forge a bond—a relationship something like his father's second marriage, solid and long-lasting, only without the commitment or the sex…

And Keir would be as safe as she could make him.

In a muted voice she said, "Thank you."

Rafe's gaze narrowed. "I don't ever want to hear that again. If I do, I'll have to thank you in return for saving my life. It could get boring."

Feeling oddly disconnected, Marisa forced a smile and retreated into the new Marisa, the one who could deal with anything. "We can't have that. Anyway, it's untrue. You were utterly determined to get out of that plane."

Her world had suddenly been shaken vigorously and turned upside down. The irony of it, she realised later in the day, was that David might not be anywhere near Tewaka so there was no need for her to put her heart in such jeopardy…

She spent the rest of the afternoon making lists of

things to do, things to buy—the most important and necessary being clothes for Keir and herself. The pile she'd brought home before the garage burned down was pathetically small.

She was also called by the insurance agent, presumably on Rafe's instructions. It was a relief to talk to him of practicalities, although the loss of her small store of treasures and mementoes was still too painful to face.

And she ironed the clothes she'd brought in, the domestic routine almost soothing her. Nadine had the day off but she always made sure there was food prepared, so after organising dinner Marisa put Keir to bed, and then, heart thumping erratically, surveyed her scanty wardrobe. In the end she chose a light shirt in a bittersweet red that somehow gave her skin a honey-coloured sheen, teeming it with a narrow pair of trousers.

"You look like a sunset," she said aloud.

For a few moments she hesitated in front of the mirror, nerves taut, then swung around and headed for the small parlour. Rafe was standing at the window, looking out over the lawn, still spring-green and lush. He turned and the banked fires in her blazed up when he smiled.

"All well?"

"Yes, he's sound asleep." She covered her strange nervousness by glancing at her watch. "Dinner should be ready in half an hour."

He indicated a tray. "Champagne is definitely appropriate for tonight. Do you like it?"

"Of course." Watching him ease the cork free, she found herself wondering dismally how often he'd done this—and for how many women.

The thought alarmed her. She'd never indulged in jealousy and she wasn't going to start now.

And the champagne was delicious.

"It comes from a vineyard I own in the South Island," he said. "Now, I have a toast."

She didn't know what to expect, smiling when he said, "To us—you, Keir and me."

Moved by the simplicity of his words, she repeated them.

Once again they ate dinner out on the terrace. Dusk fell silently and the Southern Cross emerged, diamonds on black velvet. Rafe told her more about Manuwai's fascinating history, indulging her curiosity about the place.

Marisa wondered if he knew that as each minute passed a delicious tension was building inside her.

Eventually they came inside where Rafe said calmly, "You need a ring. There's family jewellery if you'd like that, but I'll also get a jeweller to come up with a selection. I doubt if it's necessary to announce it in any newspapers—"

"Oh, no!" She went a little pale. "No, that hadn't occurred to me."

"It's possibly going to finish up in the media, just the same." Observing her dismay, he said a little tersely, "Expect some interest—and speculation—from the gossip writers, though I'll do what I can to dampen it down."

Slightly relieved, she nodded. David wouldn't read gossip columns. But when she said, "I don't need a ring", Rafe frowned.

"You do."

A note in his voice told her that need it or not, she was going to get one. After a wavering second, she decided this wasn't worth drawing a line in the sand, but she directed a challenging look at him. "Why?"

"An engagement ring means it's serious, not just a case of living together. To satisfy everyone, including your ex-husband, we need all the trimmings. And we need to do some entertaining. My friends will expect to meet you."

She tensed. "Do you think that's necessary?"

"Yes." He observed her a moment. "I hope you like them. Have you met Hani and Kelt Crysander-Gillen?"

The sudden change of subject threw her for a moment, but she shook her head. "I know of them," she said cautiously. "He's some sort of royal, isn't he, from an island in the Mediterranean?"

"No, *she*'s some sort of royal from an island in the Indian Ocean," he said with a glimmer of a smile. "Kelt's some sort of royal from a country in the Balkans, but he doesn't use his title. They live down the coast here on Kelt's station. I've known him since I was a kid. They're both extremely good company, and perfectly normal."

"Except for being royal," she said with a slight snap.

"Don't worry, they won't expect you to curtsy." When she gave a strained smile he said crisply, "You didn't have any such fears about my friend Patrick, the garage owner who fixed your car. I choose my friends for their own sakes, not because they happen to have titles. I've been called plenty of things in my time, but never a snob."

"I know you're not," she said immediately, feeling rather small. She couldn't tell him she was fighting a private battle against becoming too entrenched in his life, and that meeting his friends somehow made their agreement too personal.

His hard gaze warmed. "I'll give them a call and see if they'll come up to dinner shortly."

Marisa said politely, “That would be lovely. Do you want me to be hostess?”

Her refusal to take anything for granted irked him, but she was skittish enough without calling her on it. “Of course.” He examined her face, his body tightening when his gaze skimmed the softly full contours of her mouth.

Soon he’d take her to bed and scotch any chance of second thoughts by making her his in the most basic and simple way of all.

She might have agreed to this engagement to protect young Keir, but she’d made no attempt to deny that the attraction between them was mutual.

Rafe sometimes thought he’d been born a cynic. If he had, it had been reinforced by his mother’s abandonment. Certainly he doubted that love—the romantic, transcendent passion poets eulogised—really existed. He suspected it was a temporary madness and one he’d long ago accepted he wasn’t likely to succumb to.

Desire he understood, and friendship. He felt both for Marisa and, as well, he recognised and respected her protectiveness towards her son—perhaps because of the mother who’d sold him for ten million dollars.

Marisa’s kisses told him she’d be a willing and responsive lover. As well, she was a stimulating companion and she’d settled easily into life at Tewaka.

She broke into his thoughts with a coolly delivered statement. “You look like a lion eyeing up an antelope—anticipatory yet satisfied, because the lion knows its prey hasn’t got a hope of getting away. And that makes me nervous.”

Rafe threw back his head and laughed. He wasn’t going to tell her she’d nailed exactly how he was feeling.

“I wasn’t thinking in terms of predator and prey,”

he said, "and certainly not of killing anything. On the contrary, my thoughts and emotions are bordering on the lustful."

A surge of colour burned through Marisa's skin, and with it, a bold impulse. "Then why don't—?" Mortified at what she'd almost said, she clamped down on the rest.

But she couldn't pull her gaze away. Fascinated, she watched his gaze kindle as it swept her face, echoing the heat that flamed into life inside her, surging through her like a forest fire…

Fires destroy, she reminded herself and tried to breathe. But forest fires allow new life to flourish in their aftermath.

A little roughly he asked, "Are you indicating I'm being too noble by giving you time?"

Lips clamped tightly together in case she made an even greater fool of herself, she hesitated. He didn't move. Marisa's breath locked in her throat as she wavered on the brink of a momentous decision, one she couldn't take back or flee from.

If she made the wrong decision she'd regret it for the rest of her life.

If only she knew which *was* the wrong decision…

This was one thing she had to decide for herself, yet it took all her courage to follow her heart and give a swift, shy nod.

Rafe covered the distance between them in one rapid stride. He looked down and this time she met his gaze with no hint of challenge.

"Marisa?" He said it steadily, still not reaching out to her.

Why didn't he touch her? She dragged a breath into starving lungs. "What?"

"Say yes," he commanded almost harshly. At her nod, he tipped her chin. "*Say* it—but only if you feel it."

And suddenly it was all right. He did want her—as much as she wanted him.

Yet, like him, she needed the words. "I feel it. Do you?"

"Hell, *yes*," he said fiercely and at last caught her to him and held her there, burying his face in her hair as his grip strengthened and his body became hard against her.

She made a muffled noise in her throat and turned her face up in invitation—one he had no hesitation in accepting.

This time there was no holding back. Rafe kissed her as though he'd been starving for her since they'd first met. The thought flashed across Marisa's mind, only to be immediately banished by the force of his passion, powerful and demanding and everything she wanted.

His arms tightened around her, bringing her against his hips. Responding instantly to their blatant thrust, she gasped his name as he lifted his head and looked down at her, his narrowed gaze intent and gleaming.

"I know how to shut that quick mouth of yours now," he said on a raw note.

"Don't you dare—"

Rafe laughed so deeply she felt it reverberate through her and realised with shock that nothing like this had happened before to her.

"I like to see those green eyes light up like smouldering emeralds," he murmured, his sensuous mouth an inch from hers. "What am I not to dare?"

She had to think, reassemble her thoughts from passionate confusion. "Kissing me might stop me talking, but only while it lasts," she said clumsily, pursuing this because something told her it was important.

His eyes narrowed even further. "I know that," he said quietly. "I am not your ex-husband, Marisa. I value you for the person you are."

Value. A cold, unemotional word compared to love, yet to have Rafe value her was precious. She stiffened.

Love? Stunned, she realised what she wanted.

Rafe's love…for ever.

Because somewhere, sometime, she'd fallen in love with him. How had it happened so quickly, sneaking up on her like a silent-footed predator?

Ambushed by love, she thought half-hysterically. And this was no fly-by-night passion.

Yes, she wanted Rafe, but she loved him for other things—his surprising kindness, the unyielding determination that had got them to the hut, even his intimidating authority.

Her newfound love burned deep inside her, a steady flame that would stay alive for the rest of her life. And one day, perhaps, Rafe might learn to love her. If he didn't…

For a moment she quailed, but forced herself to face the chance of a future without Rafe.

"Get that damned man out of your head," he commanded, the words hard and short.

Marisa rallied. If he didn't learn to love her, she'd cope.

But it would hurt some secret, essential part of her for the rest of her life.

Her uplifted glance told her he expected an answer. Revealing her love for him would be a humiliation she didn't think she could bear, yet she had to bite back the words. They were going into this as equals and she wanted it to stay that way. Confessing to a hopeless love might well wreck their relationship; certainly it would alter the balance of power and put her in an inferior position.

See, you don't really trust him, something cowardly and treacherous whispered at the back of her mind.

"He's not there. I value you too," she said helplessly.

He nodded, but she sensed a subtle withdrawal, an aloofness that fled when he kissed her again and that rapturous fire took her over, mind and body.

Looking around, he said, "We can't make love here. I refuse to make love to you on a sofa."

Marisa laughed huskily and tried to cover her total surrender by muttering, "I feel like a secondary-school kid in a car."

"Not my style, even then."

She wavered, feeling uncommonly like a guilty schoolgirl. He looked down at her and laughed again, and she relaxed and smiled at him. "Nor mine," she said.

"My room."

Rafe's bedroom was huge. And beautiful.

Even living amidst the gracious beauty that was Manuwai, she hadn't expected this. The house was filled with delightful things chosen over the years by people whose wealth was restrained by discernment and taste. There was no striving to impress, no overt opulence or display emphasising wealth and power.

Rafe's room was different, although she couldn't quite put a finger on it. It breathed sophistication from the huge French sleigh bed on a shallow dais, its frame glowing with the polish and loving care of at least a century, to the massive armoire on one wall and the opulent curtains and silk bedcover.

Yet it was oddly impersonal and so far from her experience she hesitated, then stopped.

"It's overwhelming, I know."

She flinched at Rafe's accurate deduction.

He continued, "Apart from the bed, my mother—my birth mother, that is—had it redecorated when she married my father. When she left he moved out, but I like the outlook so I took it over when I was eighteen or so."

Marisa swallowed. "It's very lovely."

His hand light on her arm, he turned her around so the huge bed no longer dominated her field of vision and surveyed her with an expression she couldn't read, his boldly chiselled features impassive. "I hear another *but* coming and you're right. It's expensive and over the top—like my mother, I believe."

"I love that bed," she said swiftly. "And the armoire."

"Are you having second thoughts?"

"Not about you," she said, then stopped, furious with herself. She'd vowed never to be vulnerable to another man, yet here she was, blushing like a virgin.

She swallowed and started again, trying hard to be cool and confident. "Are you and your mother in contact?"

His face could have won him a fortune at poker. "I haven't seen her since she walked out," he said distantly. "A few years ago she got in touch through a lawyer; she'd run through the money she sold me for and needed more."

Marisa opened her mouth, then cut short the impulsive words.

He answered her unspoken question. "I made her an allowance." His mouth twisted. "As much as she needs, not as much as she wanted."

Marisa thought of the boy—barely older then Keir—whose mother had walked away from him and turned into his arms, impulsively hugging him. "Do you hate her?"

"In a way it's worse—I feel nothing for her," he said levelly, pulling her closer. "I saw very little of her even when she lived here. When my father remarried several years later Jane was far more of a mother to me than the one who actually bore me." He shrugged. "You won't have to worry about a mother-in-law. Believe me, she isn't ever likely to want to establish contact."

The last word was a caress against her lips and then his mouth took hers, warmly seductive and very persuasive. Marisa went under—lost in pleasure, in excitement, in the security and sensuality of his powerful body against her.

On fire, she luxuriated in her own response as he explored her mouth and then the warm length of her throat, one hand deftly flicking open the buttons of her shirt to cup a breast. Her heart thundered in her ears, each drumbeat marking another step in her surrender.

Delight shot through her at the sinuous stroke of his fingers across the alerted tips of her breast. Like honeyed lightning, pleasure crackled across every cell in her body, mingling crazily with an erotic frustration that urged her to tug his shirt free.

More than anything she wanted to feel his skin against her palms, but the shirt refused to move.

Rafe kissed her again, a snatched, urgent kiss that was cut short when he straightened and in one smooth movement pulled the garment over his head.

He was magnificent—skin sheened coppery-gold over corded muscles as he tossed the shirt on to a chair and turned to face her again. Silken scrolls of hair joined in the middle of his chest, forming a line that plunged downwards. Dumbstruck, Marisa devoured the sight of him, then reached out a tentative finger and followed that line to the waistline of his trousers.

Mouth compressed, he froze. Clumsily, Marisa wrenched off her shirt and tossed it after his. Rafe's eyes narrowed and the ache in her became a demand, an insistence.

And then cold caution forced her to shut her eyes against him. She dragged in a breath too close to a sob and opened them again. "Rafe, we can't. I'm sorry—I didn't think. I'm not protected."

"I have protection," he said curtly. "Do you trust me to use it?"

"Yes." Her voice shook, but she held his eyes steadily.

"You make me feel a hundred metres tall."

Startled, she asked, "Why?"

"You forgot about it until now," he said and gave her a wry smile, "and although it might be arrogant of me, I can only assume you forgot it for the same reason I did."

Because she was too absorbed in the erotic enchantment of his love-making…

Nodding, she waited impatiently, but he didn't take the small step that separated them.

He was waiting for her to make the first move.

What should she do? Colour burned up through her skin, heated her face. She just didn't have what it took to stand there and strip off in front of him.

Silently he turned her with a light touch. She shivered at the feel of his fingers against her skin while he made short work of the clip before twisting her to face him again.

When she met his eyes it was all she could do to hide

a gasp. They blazed, fiercely hungry in a face that was all harshness, its bold planes and angles in high relief.

In a voice that told her how much restraint he was using, he said, "You are beautiful."

"I have stretch marks," she blurted.

He flung back his head and laughed, and before she had a chance to do more than bitterly regret her inane remark he swept her close to him and held her tight, one hand sweeping down to hold her against his aroused loins.

Headstrong hunger took her over. She shuddered at the power of it and even more when he slid his other hand between them, taking with it the zip on her trousers.

"I don't care about stretch marks," he said and kissed her again.

Sinking into pleasure she'd never before experienced, Marisa believed him.

He lifted her and carried her across to that huge bed, easing her down on to it and somehow managing to rid her of her last garments so that she lay naked on the silken cover. Still embarrassed, feeling far too much like some harem girl brought in for her master's pleasure, she closed her eyes under his scorching survey.

Until Rafe's voice caused them to fly open again.

"Look at me," he commanded. "There's no one else in this room but you and me, and I want you." He dropped his trousers and stood straight, splendid as a bronze statue of some ancient athlete. "Do you want me?"

"Yes," she said instantly, her voice sure and direct.

"Then there's no reason for you to worry about anything else," he said and came down beside her and kissed her, one clever, experienced hand slipping the length of her body to show her just how erotically disturbing this potent hunger could be.

Later she'd allow herself the voluptuous luxury of remembering how skilfully he'd coaxed her into wildness, caressing her skin and then covering it with kisses until an agony of need brought a muffled cry from her lips.

But while she experienced his lovemaking, she had no words to use, could only surrender to a raw passion that met and matched his until he said something short and terse beneath his breath and slid over her and into her, and then stopped, every muscle locked while she convulsed beneath and around him, her body in thrall to such transcendent ecstasy she almost sobbed as each wave took her further and further into satiation.

Until finally it shattered and she came down in the safety of his arms, gasping as she dragged air into her lungs.

When she looked up she whispered, "I'm so sorry…"

He frowned. "Why?"

"Because you haven't… I…" She exhaled and said, "I didn't know it could happen so fast." Or at all…

Not to her, anyway.

"Now I feel two hundred metres tall," he said and kissed her, this time with something like tenderness.

To Marisa's stunned astonishment his kiss summoned fire from the embers. She welcomed the slow backwards-and-forwards friction that gently, sensuously, stirred her into life once more. And this time she soared even higher, drowning in a tide of bliss, and almost immediately he followed her, his proud head flung up, skin gleaming as he took his pleasure in her.

When it was finished he held her close as she sank down to something approaching normalcy, her whole being lulled by a kind of radiance that almost made her weep, while their heartbeats slowed and synchronised.

Eventually Rafe said, "I wish you didn't have to leave, but I suppose sharing a bed with me is something we'll have to introduce Keir to slowly."

"Yes," she said, a little jolted at being recalled to real life again.

Would Rafe get tired of always having to consider her son? It should be reassuring to know that although love didn't come into this equation, he enjoyed sex with her.

The question nagged sufficiently for her to ask him.

He didn't hand her an automatic reply, but said after a moment's pause, "I've always had to consider other people—my sister, and the workers here and at the various interests I have around the world. I'm growing fond of Keir—he's a good kid." He moved slightly so he could see her face. "I won't resent him—because that's really what you're asking."

His perception was brutal but accurate. "Yes, I suppose so," she said with a rueful smile. "I'm glad."

"I'll be spending far more time at home than I have in the past," he said, still watching her.

Rafe rather prided himself on his ability to read faces, but Marisa's hid far more than it revealed.

However, he was sure of one thing. She'd enjoyed their lovemaking. Neither orgasm had been faked, not even the second one. His body stirred at the memory and he pushed back the tumble of honey-gold hair from her face and kissed her again.

She responded with gratifying enthusiasm, but he curbed his instinctive urge to take things further. Her shocked delight at her own capacity for passion hadn't escaped him, but he wasn't prepared to jeopardise her fragile trust by exhausting her.

Soon the news would get around and that could well flush David Brown out of whatever rat hole he was hiding in. Tomorrow he'd ginger up his investigator.

CHAPTER TWELVE

THE next day Marisa and Rafe told Keir that he was going to live at Waimanu for a while. Warily, Marisa watched her son absorb this, dark eyes going from one to the other.

Eventually he asked a little tentatively, "Will you be my dad then?"

"I'll always be your friend if you want me to be," Rafe said.

His words and the calm tone were perfect. Marisa let out a silent breath of relief when Keir flushed and beamed.

"Yes," he said exuberantly, adding with automatic politeness, "Please."

He gave another huge grin and high-fived—something he'd learned from his schoolmates. As Rafe bent to clap palms with him, relief gave Marisa's smile a buoyancy she hadn't felt for a long time.

"Yes, I do want to be your friend," Keir said positively. "Like Manu. He gave me half his banana the other day at school and he said I could come and play with him after school one day." He looked at his mother.

Marisa said, "One day, certainly." She didn't expect everything to be so simple, but his acceptance of the situation delighted her—overwhelming for a few minutes her fear that Keir would be hurt.

When he'd gone off to tell an already informed Nadine, Rafe looked at her. "Don't worry about him. Or his father. Even if he turns up, you and Keir will both be perfectly safe."

"How are you going to manage that?" she asked starkly.

"I have ways. By the way, I've warned the school," he said.

Marisa's head came up, and she stared indignantly at him. "I saw the principal in the street today."

"I see. I wish you had discussed it with me first."

"I should have," he agreed urbanely. "It won't happen again."

He reached for her, holding her in a grip that was firm and infinitely exciting.

"Relax," he said. "I know how independent you are—I admire you for that immensely—but let me deal with this, all right?"

Trying to relax, she said, "I'll let you get away with that this time, but don't think it will work every time."

He laughed and kissed her, and for a few precious moments she could forget everything.

Until Keir's voice intruded. "Manu said his parents kiss all the time," he announced from behind them. "Are you going to too?"

Marisa jerked, but Rafe held her in a firm grip. "Quite a lot," he said. "Why?"

Wrinkling his nose, Keir said, "'Cause it looks funny." He switched his gaze to Rafe. "Manu said you can ride like the best jockey in the world. Can you show me so I can ride too? Manu said you still have the horse that showed you how to ride."

"I have," Rafe said, releasing an intensely relieved Marisa.

Clearly her son was going to use Manu's parents as an exemplar for their relationship. Nothing of possessiveness had showed in his voice and her spirits soared.

"Sammy is too old for anyone to ride now," Rafe continued. "I'll put you up on another horse. Then if you still want to learn to ride, we can see about finding a pony for you."

While Marisa was warily digesting this, Keir bounced with excitement. "Now?"

The telephone rang and Rafe said easily, "No, not now. This is an important call and I'll take this in my office."

As he left the room Keir grumbled, "I don't like that telephone. I want to ride."

"You heard Rafe. He'll take you for a ride when he can. Let's go and see if any birds have found the feeder we made yesterday yet."

But as they went out Marisa felt a cold finger of foreboding down her spine.

It took three days for Rafe to be able to fulfil his promise, and neither he nor Marisa had been allowed to forget it.

Marisa was surprised at how well it went. That afternoon Keir had been allowed to come home on the school bus with Manu and play at his house. She'd collected him after shutting up the shop and he was still buzzing about it. However, he obeyed instantly when Rafe warned him to speak quietly because it might spook the little brown mare.

Watching a little anxiously, Marisa was impressed by Rafe's patience and expertise.

"I should know what I'm doing," he said coolly when she commented on it. "My father put me up on a horse before I could walk and I watched him teach Gina to ride."

"I have to say the horse is extremely patient." They had made love the previous night and she had not been patient at all during the two other nights. Although she tried to convince herself she was imagining things, that odd sense of disconnection was still between them, as though he was building a wall against her.

"That's why I chose her," he said. "She's very sweet-tempered."

Keir was clearly enjoying himself, frowning with concentration as he listened, and instantly obeying each of Rafe's instructions.

"He has good balance and no fear," Rafe observed when the ten minutes he'd allotted for the first lesson was over. He looked at Marisa. "Do you ride?"

"This is probably the closest I've ever been to a horse."

Rafe asked, "Are you afraid of them?"

"Only in as much as they're a lot bigger than I am and I have no idea how they think."

"If you like," he said casually, "I'll take you on as a pupil too."

It was said lightly enough, but something in his tone alerted her, adding to her creeping apprehension.

Something had definitely changed. It was too subtle for her to put a finger on, but every sense was on full alert, stretched so tight she felt light-headed. He seemed to have withdrawn, revealing nothing but the most superficial of feelings and making polite chitchat as though she were a visitor, not the woman with whom he'd made wild and uninhibited love the previous night.

Her cheeks grew warm at the memory. Now she knew just how reckless she could be, how her body could sing under his skilful hands and turn to fire…

"Marisa?"

"Oh," she said, startled. Her colour deepened and she said swiftly, "Yes, I think I would like it, thank you."

When she looked up his gaze kindled, was shielded by thick black lashes, but he said merely, "Fine. But if Keir's to have his dinner on time, it's time to go."

Later, when Keir had been put to bed, she walked along to the terrace where they normally had dinner. Rafe wasn't there, and that elusive apprehension abraded her nerves once more.

The housekeeper came in. "Ah, there you are. Rafe said to tell you he's riding and he'll be later than usual tonight. Shall I get you a drink?"

"No, thanks." Marisa paused before asking, "Where does he ride?"

"He's gone along the beach. Usually that means he needs to think through something. If you walk out to the summerhouse you'll probably see him coming back." Nadine smiled affectionately. "I think he misses playing polo. He had to give it up after his father died because he was so busy."

The summerhouse was placed to take in a view of the long sweep of the ocean beach. Cicadas shrilled their high-pitched wooing calls—like miniature buzz-saws, Marisa thought as she took up the binoculars kept there and focused them on the horse and rider in the distance. Her heart thudded when she noted great clumps of wet sand flying from the big gelding's hooves.

It couldn't be as dangerous as it looked.

And Rafe was obviously a superb horseman, moving as one with the animal. When they came closer she could see his face, purposeful and set as though he'd made a difficult decision.

She waited until horse and rider left the beach, then ambled back to the house, enjoying the scents and sounds of summer. A stray bee buzzed around her head before zooming off like a golden bullet in the sunlight towards a bush humming with other nectar-seekers.

She loved this garden. *Face it, you love everything about Manuwai—the house, the beaches, even the workers you've met so far...*

And she'd give it all up if the man who owned it decided he no longer wanted to live here.

She'd been told love was all-encompassing, and during the short time since Rafe had entered her life again, she'd learned that it was true, there were no limits to it.

How long she walked in the muted light of early evening she didn't know. Questions—most of them unanswerable—beat her bluntly like physical blows.

Was Rafe regretting their engagement? Pierced by pain, she faltered. Whatever happened, she'd deal with it. But she'd never be the same again.

And coping seemed a dreary way to spend the rest of her life.

You'd have Keir...

It hurt to admit it, but her son was no longer enough. She was a woman and Rafe had woken her to her full potential.

She stopped beside the vivid flowers of a tropical rhododendron, so blazingly golden they were incandescent in the soft light. They dazzled her eyes and brought tears to them.

Was that all it was? Sex?

No, she loved Rafe for what he was, not just because he made her feel a rapturous certainty in his arms.

And she'd had this conversation with herself before. She had to stop going obsessively over and over the same worries, the same concerns.

A sixth sense lifted the hair on the back of her neck. She swivelled and saw him watching her. Something she saw in his face brought an icy wave of fear.

"You'd better tell me," she said harshly.

If anything, his face hardened even more. "Walk with me to the summerhouse."

Once there, she met unreadable eyes, burnished and brutal as the barrel of a gun. Voice shaking, she demanded, "What is it?"

"David Brown is dead."

The words fell like bombs into the still, salt-fragrant air. *"W-what?"* she stammered, her legs shaking so much he caught her.

Only for a moment. As though he no longer wanted to touch her, he lowered her into one of the chairs and stepped back, turning slightly to look out to sea before he spoke.

"He died this afternoon on the road here." No emotion was evident in his cool, judicial tone. "You know that steep patch through bush just before you come out on to the coast? He was driving too fast to take the corner. He drove straight over the edge on to the rocks below. He'd have died instantly."

She flinched, imagining the fall—the terror and the pain. And then oblivion…

Tears burned behind her eyes. Whatever she had feared, she had never wanted this. "Thank heaven for that at least," she said unevenly. "I'm glad he didn't suffer. It's horrible to be so—so relieved, but I d-didn't want him to die. But—he was coming here?"

"No, speeding away. It looks as though he was waiting for Keir to come home in the school bus with Manu." He paused as she dragged in a sharp breath and turned blindly towards the house. Roughly he said, "It's all right, Marisa. He's still in bed, still asleep. I've just checked."

That stopped her. After a short hesitation she turned back to him and said harshly, "How do you know this?"

"I had someone keeping an eye on both you and Keir." He saw her blink at that, but she said nothing, and he went on, "Yesterday she noticed a man in a car who seemed very interested in the children leaving school. When she phoned the details through she found the vehicle had been bought by Brown in Auckland a month ago."

Struggling to control her distress, she asked, "But how did David know Keir would be on the bus today?"

Rafe quelled an instinctive desire to comfort her. Better to get the ugly truth done with first. "He was there again today, watching Keir get on to the bus with Manu. He left then and my investigator stayed with the bus, following it. When they reached Waimanu he was waiting, but as soon as he saw her drive up he took off. She followed and he took the corner too fast and went over on to the rocks."

He restrained himself from telling her that his investigator had unearthed enough information for him to be very concerned about the reappearance of David Brown.

White-faced, she stared at him, absorbing the implications. "No, that won't fit. He didn't know Keir was his son. Even if he had been, he wouldn't have been interested..." Her voice trailed away and her gaze narrowed, became accusing. "You know more than you're telling me."

She had to know sooner or later. It might as well be sooner. "The garage at the Tanners' place *was* deliberately set on fire and his car was seen on the road close by that night."

"But if he was following Keir, he must have had plans for him too," she said thinly.

"We'll never know. Possibly he was finding out where I lived so he could set fire to something else."

She refused to accept his false comfort. "But you don't believe that."

He shook his head. "I don't know. Nobody will ever know. Leave it at that."

Visibly gathering strength, Marisa straightened her shoulders. Sombrely she said, "I suppose when he found out I'd moved to Tewaka, he'd have thought I'd chosen it because you live here."

"Almost certainly." When she shivered, he said brusquely, "You realise that his death has freed you from any need to be concerned about Keir's future?"

She stared at him, her eyes too darkly shadowed for him to guess at her thoughts.

So that was it.

Marisa tried to speak but her throat was too dry. He was telling her she could go. She had to swallow before she could say, "Yes, I do." Moving carefully, like an old woman, she got to her feet. "Then I have to thank you for...for everything. Keir and I will move out as soon as I can organise it."

Stone-faced, he said, "You don't have to." He paused, then added curtly, "I'd like you to stay. But if you want to go, then of course you must."

Marisa looked away, pride fighting a losing battle with need. *Tell him*, she urged herself. *Tell him you don't want to go—then at least you'll know...*

But cowardice kept her silent.

Almost aggressively Rafe asked, "Do you want to go, Marisa?"

She stiffened her spine and looked directly at him, and took the biggest gamble of her life. "No, I do not. I want to stay here and marry you and have your children—if—"

Her voice broke on a sob.

After one short, explicit word under his breath, he grabbed her—*grabbed* her, her cool Rafe, always so self-sufficient, so confident—and hauled her against him as though he would never let her go.

"I knew I loved you when you made those conditions for our engagement," he said unsteadily.

Joy burst through her, a nova of delight and relief and pleasure. Trembling, she asked, "Why? I thought they'd put you off."

He didn't kiss her. Instead his arms clamped around her and he said unsteadily in a raw, formidable voice, "You were prepared to set me free without any recriminations if I met someone I could love and I thought, *I've already met her.* Before that I wanted you—your eyes caught my attention in Mariposa and when I saw you again I got a shock of recognition, as though I've been marking time since then, waiting for you."

"I know," she whispered, filled with a joy so palpable she felt she could fly. "Oh, yes, I know exactly how you felt—it was just like that for me too."

Eyes kindling, he looked down into her face. "But I had no idea how *much* I loved you until I heard of Brown's death. I've been through hell, afraid you'd leave once you knew any danger to Keir was over." He took in a sharp, impeded breath. "Damn it, Marisa, how do you feel about me? I need the words."

"I love you, of course. Surely you must know that?" she cried. "I think I must have started to love you when we met in Mariposa—before then I'd been that drab, miserable shell of a woman, but you arrived like a storm—like rain after drought. I'd been so passive, so—so *useless*—and somehow—by just being *you*—you forced me to realise that if I wanted to get away, I had to fight for it. And I did. I told David that I was going home whether he wanted me to or not."

"And you did," he said with immense satisfaction and at long last bent his head and kissed her.

Later that night, lying in Rafe's arms, she thought dreamily that she was where she belonged. Her parents had loved her, but they'd wanted a daughter like them, a gypsy at heart, and David had tried to force her to become whatever he'd wanted…

She hoped he'd found peace at last.

As she had. Along with passion and laughter and the sweet torment of love, she had found a home. Rafe was everything she'd wanted without even realising it and he accepted her as she was; with him she could be her true self.

"Going to sleep?" His voice was rough and tender at the same time. "When are you going to marry me?"

She yawned and turned over and kissed his shoulder. "How soon can we get married?" she murmured.

Rafe laughed, the low, triumphant laugh of a lover. "We can probably get married within a month." He paused, and then said in a voice she'd never heard before, "I've been so sure I could never lose my head over a woman, that I simply didn't have it in me to fall in love, and then you moved in and I fell before I understood what the hell had hit me."

"You and me both," she told him with love and a sense of utter commitment, and ran her hand down his chest.

"I love you," he said deeply. "I'll love you for the rest of my life."

"And I love you and always will."

Their wedding would come in time, but both knew those words marked their pledge to each other.

Rafe kissed her, murmuring against her mouth, "Tired?"

"I thought I was," she purred, running her hand across his chest, "but I seem to have new lease of life…"

He smiled. "Me too."

And together, confidently, they embarked on their future.

* * * * *

Special Offers
Lynne Graham Collection

An intense and passionate collection of international bestselling author Lynne Graham's trademark powerful, hot-blooded heroes

Collect all 4 volumes!

On sale 3rd February

On sale 2nd March

On sale 6th April

On sale 4th May

Save 20% on Special Releases Collections

Find out more at
www.millsandboon.co.uk/specialreleases

Visit us Online

0312/52/MB365